MAHOGANY RED BOOKS PRESENTS

Pink
SHADES
of
seduction

A NOVEL BY
HAZEL MILLS

Delphine Publications focuses on bringing a reality check to the genre Published by Delphine Publications

Delphine Publications focuses on bringing a reality check to the genre urban literature. All stories are a work of fiction from the authors and are not meant to depict, portray, or represent any particular person Names, characters, places, and incidents are either the product of the author's imagination or are used fictitiously, and any resemblances to an actual person living or dead are entirely coincidental

ISBN: 978-1519759665

Layout: Write On Promotions
Cover Design: Odd Ball Designs

Shades of Pink Seduction

A LOVER IS BORN

I needed to get the fuck out of town! Work had been kicking my ass for the past few months. When I decided to become a psychiatrist, I knew I wouldn't have a lot of free time to enjoy the money I would make. However, I never imagined it would be this hectic. Case after case of bipolar disorders, schizophrenia and ADHD was making me lose my mind. Gabe and I both needed immediate rest and relaxation.

Five years ago, we purchased a country cottage and renovated it. As well as it being a place where we could escape from the city scene, the house was to be our own private little love nest.

Gabe and I met ten years ago at a book club discussion that my receptionist held once a month at her house. Even though I couldn't find much time to read the monthly selections, I enjoyed the camaraderie and conversations. The group was a gumbo of people of all ages and backgrounds: housewives, a teacher, a veterinarian and a marketing professor. One member, who was a sommelier for one of the city's upscale hotels, would bring excellent wines for us to taste and, of course, we happily obliged. We would just chill and enjoy each other, while catching up on the latest gossip. Gabe was one of the few people in the group who actually read the monthly selection and looked forward to discussing its every detail. Although the book discussion only lasted for about an hour, we would eat, drink and be merry for far longer.

Albeit we weren't formally introduced, there was something electric between Gabe and me, something strong that we both felt. We exchanged long glances and shy smiles during the evening and defended each other's points of view. There was always so much going on during the discussions, yet we never had a chance to chat one on one. I wanted, and needed, to know more about that intriguing character and it wasn't long before the perfect opportunity presented itself.

The club members were trying to decide on a venue for our Christmas party. We wanted to reserve the private dining room at an exclusive Japanese restaurant but were late in planning that year's event and the place was booked solid. Therefore, I suggested having the party at my house. Besides, the refurbishing of my 19th Century brownstone uptown was completed and I wanted to show it off. Everyone agreed so I dusted off my hosting skills. I had not hosted a party in a very long time and had grossly underestimated the amount of work involved. However, I was glad I could afford to call in reinforcement, if needed, and it would be worth every cent if Gabe and I hooked up afterwards. Plus, since there was no book to discuss that month, Gabe and I would be able to talk and get to know each other much better. Hosting the party on my own turf made me more confident and Gabe was my prey.

Planning the party to be an evening of casual elegance, I hired an excellent caterer to serve a menu of culinary delights. As a favor, my designer had the house filled with beautiful red poinsettias and a Christmas tree that rivaled the one at Rockefeller Center. As the guests were arriving, I realized that all of that elaborateness would have been in vain had Gabe not shown up. But, I didn't have to worry about that because just as I was about to give up hope, the doorbell rang, and it was Gabe.

"Merry Christmas and welcome to my home. I'm Laila," I greeted.

"Feliz Navidad. I'm Gabriella."

I couldn't believe she was actually in my home. My heart raced as I considered the possibilities that the evening held.

Gabe walked graciously inside followed by an intoxicating aura of Chanel No.22. Truly the most beautiful woman I had ever seen, Gabe made Halle Berry look like Shaq in drag. With her hair pulled back into a sexy ponytail, as tendrils dangled around her face, her caramel skin glowed flawlessly in the candlelight.

"Come in. I'll take your coat."

"Gracias. Thank you. Let me say that you have a spectacular home." She walked slowly through the foyer, admiring the eclectic mix of art and antiques. "How long have you lived here?"

"Oh, about three years."

I watched her tall slender form stroll effortlessly from room to room, peaking inside. Damn she was fine!

"Come into the parlor and say hello to everyone, get a drink and have a look around," I encouraged.

The party went off without a hitch. Everyone enjoyed sitting down at the two large round tables in the dining room and eating a traditional gourmet Christmas dinner by the fire. As we laughed and talked all evening, I was aroused by the mere sound of Gabe's voice. She reminded me of a Latina Demi Moore. I learned that she was divorced. She worked as a detective and her husband couldn't handle it. He was content when she was a beat cop but when she became a detective and her work had grown intense, things quickly deteriorated. They didn't have any children, so once the ties were severed they were severed for good. I also found out that her family was originally from Puerto Rico. They moved to Miami when she was five and then here, to Brooklyn, when she was in high school. I followed her around like a puppy all evening.

Gabe and a few others lingered on a while after the party for a rousing game of bid whist. But, after a couple hours of that, there was only Gabe left. She offered to stay and help with some of the cleanup. I knew there was no real reason for her to help with anything because Chandra, my housekeeper, was due that next morning but I welcomed the opportunity to have her all to myself. We continued to laugh and talk about everything while cleaning and then, there it was. That awful awkward silent moment that we all hate and that few people know what to do with.

Knowing that Gabe had been married made me a little concerned about whether or not she would even be down for what I had in mind. There was only one way to find out.

"Gabe, may I ask you a personal question?" I moved closer to where she stood.

"Sure. Go ahead."

"Are you dating anyone right now?"

I hoped that after asking that question, I wouldn't have to listen to her go on and on about some fine ass man on the force that she was head over hills in love with.

"No. Unfortunately not. I haven't dated a lot since the divorce. Once most men find out what I do for a living, their balls shrink."

I laughed and decided to move on to the next question. "How do you feel about women?"

Her brow rose. "What do you mean?" she asked in a suspicious tone.

"Are you into women?"

I could tell that she was not at all surprised by my curiosity. I had been out ever since medical school so virtually everyone knew that I was a lesbian. I never hid my lifestyle nor did I wear it on my sleeve. I just lived my life. My last lover was still in the closet and wasn't interested in coming out anytime soon. Her husband was a minister and she wanted to avoid the extra drama, and so did I. After months of sneaking around, I realized that I deserved someone who could be open about her love for me no matter who was watching. I also wanted someone who didn't come with a ton of baggage. Life was too short to live in hiding.

Slowly raising the wine glass to her full lips, she smiled. "No one has ever asked me that before." She took another sip of wine.

Sitting my glass of wine on the countertop, I moved in closer to her, hypnotized by her deep onyx eyes. I felt as if I was looking directly into her beautiful soul. "Well, I love women. I love everything about them from the way they smell to the way they feel. I especially love the way they taste," I whispered, as I crept in closer.

"Yes, I know you do." She spoke softly while holding my stare.

Gabe never answered my question and she didn't back away. It was as if she dared me to make the next move and that shit turned me on, and the prolonged anticipation was almost unbearable.

"Do you realize how very beautiful you are right now?"

As she parted her luscious lips to say, "Thank you," I gently pressed my French manicured fingertip against her mouth, before covering it with mine. I gently kissed her soft, full lips and then, as if instinctively, she opened her mouth and welcomed my tongue. We kissed, our tongues dancing in celebration of what was to come.

"You are breathtaking," I said softly while gently stroking her cheek.

"Toma mi respira lejos, tambien."

"What does that mean?" I was a little turned on by the Spanish.

"It means that you take my breath away, too."

We kissed again deeply, I explored her body with my hands, touching her firm breasts, rubbing my thumb against her already hard nipples through her silk blouse and she closed her eyes, slowly gasping with pleasure.

Slightly pulling back, yet not breaking our embrace, she said, "I've never loved a woman before. I hope my inexperience doesn't disappoint you."

"Do what comes naturally and let your body respond to my touch."

Gently stoking a growing fire, she held me tight around the waist, pulling me closer. Not even a vaguely sensuous light could have passed between us. We were breathing hard and fast—her breath was warm and moist against my face—sensuously pawing and groping, undressing each other. I was amazed at how quickly Gabe had removed my blouse and bra, setting my titties free with what seemed like one smooth motion. Caressing my breasts in the palm of her hands, she kissed each one before kneeling down to pull my skirt down around my ankles, leaving me standing there wearing only a smile.

"Eres mas hermosa que una manana en el verano."

"What?"

"You are more beautiful than a summer morning," Gabe cooed.

I could tell she worked out. Her body was tight. Her breasts stood like two party hats and her ass was so firm, I could have bounced a quarter off it. Her skin was as soft as a yellow rose. It was like butta baby! I reached between her legs to feel her dripping like a faucet, waiting to be turned on full force.

Wanting to move that party to my bedroom, and without a word, I took Gabe's hand and led her upstairs, and, as her smile sent my pulses racing, she willingly followed. We both knew where that was going and couldn't wait to get there.

After lighting a few candles, we climbed into my bed and held each other for a while, stroking and caressing. I started kissing her breasts, taking them inside my mouth, almost swallowing them whole. I suckled at her nipples like an infant and then encircled them with my tongue like a lover. She expelled a moan that came from deep within.

"That's it, baby. Let me make you feel good," I instructed.

Wanting to feel the warmth of her insides, I gently thumbed her swollen clitoris while teasing her hot opening with my fingertip. And, sensing she was on the verge of euphoria, I slid my fingers in and out of her wetness, causing her to buck like a horse. She rode my hand until she came like a freight train and made almost as much noise. Her pussy muscles gripped my fingers and sucked them for more. Licking my fingers, I tasted her sweet sap. She tasted wonderful!

Gabe couldn't wait to return the pleasure, as she kissed me, letting her tongue explore every inch of my mouth, before moving down to my neck licking and sucking until she found my spot and lingered there for what seemed like an eternity. The thrill that shot through my body was electrifying. She continued her trip down my entire body, like a tourist looking for her favorite attraction. She finally made it to my ultimate pleasure point and I gladly opened my legs wider, giving her full access. She then buried her head deep into my rainforest. I writhed and moaned as she worked her voodoo on my clit with her tongue. That woman had me totally under her spell, as I sat up a little because I had to watch the artist at work. Her eyes were closed and she was oblivious to anything other than my pleasure. Never have I had someone so into me as she, and I loved it, and deserved it. I ran my fingers through her dark tresses that blanketed my stomach as she greedily ate me, dousing euphoria on an already burning fire. I grabbed her head and pushed it deeper into my damp muff as I came harder than ever, screaming her name for the world to hear. Gabe kissed her way up just as she had kissed her way down, which made me tremble with aftershock. We fell asleep together, basking in complete satisfaction.

The sun rose on our lovemaking the next morning. I introduced Gabe to Venus, my double dildo. After a quick crash course on how to use it, we glided ourselves onto it and went for a fabulous ride. We lay face to face and gyrated on its hardness, breathing each other's breath and watching the waves of ecstasy in each other's eyes. Holding on for dear life, we were overcome by earth shattering orgasms that seemed to last for days.

Now, here we are, ten years later and deeper in love. I can truly say that Gabriella is my soul mate and I look forward to spending forever with her.

ABOVE THE LAW

Damn, I thought when I saw the red and blue lights flashing in the rearview mirror of my Mercedes. This was the third time that I had been pulled over for speeding this month and I knew that neither my husband nor my insurance company would be too pleased if I were to receive another speeding ticket. I had to figure out a way to get off with just a warning this time and it had to be with a better excuse than the usual "I'm late for work" story I had used so many times before. I tried to calm myself as I pulled over on the side of the dusty country road. The tall officer climbed out of his cruiser and sternly walked over to the open driver's side window of my car. Turning on the charm was going to be easy.

"Hello Officer," I smiled, seductively parting my lips.

"Do you realize how fast you were going, Ma'am?" Through his dark sunglasses, he gazed into my hazel brown eyes. From the slight tilt of his head, I gathered he directed his attention to my ample chest that was barely hidden beneath a white linen blouse. I got a good look at him, too. He looked like a giant chocolate bar wrapped in blue cellophane. His tight uniform showed off his large, perfectly sculpted body, while his form fitting pants bulged at the zipper, making me eager to play with his concealed weapon. The dry July heat was causing tiny beads of sweat to dance on his delicious dark, baldhead.

Seductively pouting, I licked the edges of my glossed lips. "I know I fractured the speed limit a little, officer but if you would just give me a warning, I promise to be more careful in the future," I lied, knowing I had him once he saw my nipples hardening under his lustful gaze.

Smiling devilishly, as his tongue stroked his full bottom lip. "Perhaps we can work something out."

"Perhaps," I paused, parting my shapely brown thighs a little more, allowing my skirt to rise above my thick luscious thighs, revealing the absence of my panties. "Do you know of a more suitable place where we can go and work something out?"

As the corners of his mouth curled up into a seductive smile, exposing a beautiful row of pearly whites, he nodded his head toward his cruiser. "Follow me."

Following him to an old dairy farm two miles down the road, we parked behind a deserted red barn that still had bales of hay inside. As soon as I opened my car door, the fiery heat of an Alabama summer beat down on me like a drum.

I quickly turned around as the gravel beneath his feet alerted me to his approach.

"Now, what were you saying about working something out?" he asked.

Eagerly, I led him into the stuffy barn. I smiled as I reached out and massaged his already hard dick through his pants. He threw his head back and let out a soulful sigh of ecstasy. When I knelt down in front of him and unzipped his tight pants, his thickness sprung forward like a jack-in-the-box that already oozed with excitement. He wasn't wearing underwear either and I couldn't believe how much it turned me on. I licked his swollen head before I took him into my mouth, deeper and deeper until I could feel him touching the back of my throat. The scent of his sex, mixed with the subtleness of his woodsy cologne, made me dizzy with desire. I jerked and sucked him at the same time. His moans became more beastly as he pumped his cock in and out of my hot mouth. While he caressed my hard nipples through my blouse, I hummed with pleasure and that vibration seemed to excite him even more.

"You have to let me fuck you or the deal is off," he said, as he withdrew from my mouth.

Wiping the edges of my mouth, I stared him in the eyes. "Of course."

I couldn't wait to have him burrowed deep inside my marsh. Feeling frisky, I slowly undressed before him, giving him a show he would never forget. I watched him grow harder with anticipation, as he smiled slyly at the sight of my neatly shaved pussy.

I jumped on the bale of hay behind me and spread my legs wide to give Officer Friendly a better look. Before I let him inside, I wanted him to watch me pleasure myself. I leaned back and closed my eyes. Slowly, I stroked my clit, purring with delight. As I slid my fingers deep inside my wetness, waves of orgasm rolled though me. When I opened, he was completely naked and jerking off as he watched me writhe my naked ass on the hay.

I walked over to him and inserted put my cum-soaked fingers into his mouth, giving him taste my savory juices, and what was to come.

"We can take this ride together, officer. But let me drive," I said.

Taking him by the hand, I led him the bale of hay and watched as he sprawled his muscular body on the hay, in anticipation for one hell of a trip. Straddling him, I slowly lowered myself onto his dark granite, taking care to enjoy every inch. We moaned in unison as he filled me completely. My movements were slow and deliberate, as the officer laid on his back in total bliss. He wrapped his hot hands around my ass and pushed up inside me, in motion with my grinding hips. Leaning forward, my hard nipples dangled in his face, teasing him. Instinctively, he opened his mouth and received them, licking them first, then sucking and feeding on them like a baby; making me flood even more. It seemed as if the barn and everything around us was on fire as I picked up the pace and rode him with everything I had. Each thrust of his pole inside me felt like flashes of lightening causing me to shake uncontrollably. I exploded and locked my pussy muscles on his throbbing dick like a vice. Almost immediately, I felt his body stiffen as he filled me with his hot load. I came again, harder.

After we both got dressed, the officer said that I was free to go on my way.

"I would hate for you to get fired for being late for work," he said.

"Work? I wasn't on my way to work. I was going to meet my husband for lunch. I'd better hurry. Don't want that man waiting too long," I replied as I sped away.

LOVE'S SILVER LINING

April 4, 1968. The day Black America mourned the loss of our most profound leader, the man who was leading us to the Promised Land. And, on that day, I mourned the loss of a greater man who made every day of my life feel like the Promised Land. My husband, Reese, lost his battle with cancer that day. The world, as I knew it, would never be the same again.

I met Reese when I was a nursing student at Howard University. My sorority hired him to photograph our Founder's Day celebration. When he walked into the room, dressed in a navy blue pinstriped suit that flawlessly fit his tall and slender frame, my heart skipped several beats. An air of confidence surrounded him like the rings of Saturn and his golden skin shined like the sun. He had what we called back then "good hair," short and wavy. He spoke barely above a whisper as he directed us on where to sit, stand and pose. I knew it was inappropriate for me to approach him but I had to know more about the beautiful man who stole my breath. Therefore, I did a little investigating. I found out that he loved to photograph the cherry blossom trees that bloomed near the Jefferson Memorial. I happened to be there one afternoon and he asked if he could take my picture as I sat reading a book beneath one of the trees. I agreed and that was the beginning of our love affair. Reese and I didn't date. He courted me, writing me the most beautiful love letters when he was away working. We took long walks along the Potomac River, holding hands and stargazing into each other's eyes. Knowing I had a sweet tooth as long as the Mississippi River, he would bring chocolates or pralines every time he'd visit.

We were married the day after my graduation. We worked hard and bought our first home together. It was like heaven on earth, until Reese was diagnosed with lung cancer in 1966. Vowing to fight it with all that we had, nothing was going to keep us from growing old together and traveling the world with our two daughters. I quit my job at the hospital and stayed home to care for him as only I could. Even though Reese was a strong and determined man, the cancer was stronger.

He died in my arms, just as the sun rose in the sky that crisp spring morning. I laid there with him for hours. I locked the door and refused to allow anyone into the room, including our daughters, until Reese and I had said our good-byes. It seemed only right that he should die on the bed where we'd first made love. We talked over all of life's events on that bed. Our children were conceived there.

After the paramedics took his body away, I dragged the mattress out into the backyard and set it afire. In fact, I burned everything that belonged to Reese: clothes, papers, everything. My mother tried in vain to convince me to donate his things to charity instead. She said that some poor unfortunate soul could use them. I didn't care about some poor soul. There was no other man in the universe worthy to walk in Reese's shoes. The pain of losing the only man I thought I would ever love consumed and burned my soul. Cancer took Reese and part of me was gone, too.

After my husband's death, I moved back home to Birmingham to live with my mother. It was an adjustment for all of us but we made it work. I threw myself completely into my new job. My mother was a housekeeper for a wealthy white doctor and his family. He agreed to give me a job as a nurse's aide in his practice even though I had more education, and was more qualified, than the white nurses I assisted. I was a widowed Black woman, living with my mother and two daughters, working in a doctor's office with all white patients in 1969 Alabama. Reese had died and I had gone to hell.

I continued to raise the girls just as Reese would have wanted, making sure they both were college educated. They have grown into the most amazing women. Reese would be so proud if he could see them now. Our oldest, Lily, was a kindergarten teacher. Iris married and worked as a mortgage banker for a few years. After the birth of her second child, she and her husband decided that it was important that she stayed at home with the children.

Over the next four decades, my life took several detours from the path I wanted to travel. My mother died of pneumonia in 1975. Next to losing Reese, that was one of the most devastating events of my life. She had been my solid rock through everything. What becomes of an only child when her mother dies? Even though I was thirty-five when mama died, I felt like an orphan that had been left behind.

My oldest daughter Lily decided that I needed to get out more and meet new people. I tried in vain to convince her that between God, the Church and our family, I had all the people in my life that I needed. However, she insisted on enrolling me in a ballroom dance class for, as she put it, people my age. She said that I needed to be more active. This was the same thing she'd said when she enrolled me in a photography class, golf lessons and yoga for seniors.

"Mama, you just can't sit around the house all the time. You'll waste away," Lily said.

I, of course, understood my daughter's well-meant intentions. She worried about me living alone, especially since I'd retired. Iris expressed that she and her husband wanted me to live with them. Flattered, I declined. Even though I love my daughter and adore my grandchildren, I did not have any interest in being with them twenty-four-seven. Besides, just because I lived alone didn't mean I was lonely. It was my time now. I enjoyed getting to know me. Retirement meant that I was no longer on anybody's clock and could come and go, or not, as I pleased.

I reluctantly went to the dance class only because Lily had already paid for it and I hated to see a dollar go to waste, even if it wasn't mine. There were six of us in the class and all of us appeared to have been signed up by some well-meaning relative. The dance school was owned by a married couple who decided to open it after they'd both retired from the post office. They loved to dance and were eager to teach others to master the almost forgotten art of ballroom dancing. We were all paired with a partner of similar height. At that moment, I realized that in order to dance with a partner, my body would have to be guided by the hands of another man. In thirty-eight years, no man, other than my doctor, had touched me. All my desires in that area had died with Reese. He was my one and only. I quickly became very uncomfortable and started to make up an excuse and leave.

"I promise I won't bite," a deep, velvety voice spoke.

I turned around and looked straight into the lightest brown eyes I had ever seen in my life.

"Excuse me?"

"I won't bite," he said again, smiling.

"I'm sure you won't but I don't think that this class is for me." I gathered my coat and purse.

"Now, how in the world could you possibly know that? You haven't even been here ten minutes."

"It's just, well..." I tried to come up with a polite excuse, but I obviously couldn't tell him that I'd never been touched by a man in thirty-eight years, so I closed my mouth instead.

"I'm Dumas Kennedy," he said with an out-stretched hand.

"Hi, Juanita Blackwell."

Mr. Kennedy was good-looking. He was tall and thin like Reese but without hair. His caramel head was completely bald and the florescent lights of the studio rained on his slick scalp, making the diamond stud in his ear sparkle. The neatly shaved hair on his face was a perfect blend of salt and pepper.

"Give it a chance, Mrs. Blackwell. I'll even let you lead."

I decided to stay. We both watched the instructors intensely and did our best to mimic their well-choreographed steps. The firm yet gentle touch of Dumas' hand on my lower back astounded me. He held me as if I was delicately blown glass and would break and shatter into a million pieces if he were to move his hand. He was a good dancer and we moved well together.

After class, Dumas invited me out for coffee. Reluctantly, I accepted his invitation. We sat for hours in the cafe drinking coffee and talking. Dumas' wife of thirty years had died six years ago and his daughter-in-law was responsible for his sudden interest in ballroom dancing. A retired judge, the stern and decisive manner in which he spoke was captivating. When he smiled, the dimples in his cheeks were as deep as the ocean. Dumas caused stirrings that, at first, disturbed me. I thought those feelings were long gone. It had been, after all, thirty-eight years.

We continued the next six weeks together as partners in dance class and as good friends. We spent a great deal of time together going to the movies, the museum and sailing on his boat. I enjoyed Dumas' companionship. He was a lot like Reese: kind and gentle. For the first time in years, I felt more like a woman and less like a widow.

To celebrate my birthday, Dumas called and said that he wanted to take me somewhere special for dinner. I spent hours getting ready and making sure that everything was just right. I felt like a silly teenaged girl getting ready for the prom and fussing over every detail. I usually wore my hair in a perfectly tight French roll, but tonight I decided I would let the snow-white tresses hang freely around my shoulders. The black pantsuit Iris had given me as a gift hugged my slim frame as if it were custom-made. I admired myself in the full-length mirror. I was sixty and still wore the same size as I did when I was thirty. Not many women could make that claim.

When the doorbell rang, I tied a silk zebra print scarf around my neck and ran downstairs. There was no need to keep the man waiting. I opened the door to complete surprise on Dumas' face as he held a single red rose. Speechless.

"Is that for me?" I asked, reaching for the flower.

"Of course," he said, still gazing.

"Thank you." I smelled the rose and pretended not to notice his stare.

"Juanita, you are stunning tonight."

"Just tonight?"

"Well, no. Not just tonight. You are always beautiful. There's just something different about you tonight. I can't put my finger on it."

I thought Dumas had planned to take me to an extravagant restaurant for dinner. I was wrong. We drove out to what seemed like the most remote part of the county. There were no streetlights and we rarely passed another car on the road. Only darkness. When I asked where in the hell we were going, he smiled and said that I should be patient. After a while, we turned off the main road, drove through large iron gates that seemed to anticipate our arrival and opened automatically. There was still darkness everywhere and then suddenly a huge well-lit house appeared out of nowhere. It was stately but not intimidating. Even at night, I could tell that the landscape was lush and green. The sweet smell of gardenias danced past my nose as I rose from the car. The sound of a distant fountain instantly flushed me with tranquility.

"Is this your place?" I asked Dumas, as he closed the car door.

"Yea, it is," he said, proudly.

We walked along a dimly lit stone walkway to the front porch that wrapped endlessly around the entire house. When I walked through the stained glass doors, my breath was taken away. The place was absolutely gorgeous! It was hard to believe that a bachelor lived there.

"Make yourself at home. Look around if you like," Dumas offered, as he dashed quickly into the kitchen.

Every room was an eclectic mix of things he'd collected from his travels. European antiques and African artifacts blended together perfectly. Careful attention had been paid to every decorating detail.

"You have a beautiful home, Dumas." I walked into the kitchen where he was preparing a salad.

There were pots of this and pans of that simmering on the stove, each with a bewitching aroma of something wonderful. My palette was aroused.

"I know that you expected to go out to a restaurant for dinner but I wanted to make something special for you with my own hands."

Dumas was a fabulous cook and dinner was delicious. He explained how he'd called Lily and found out that one of my favorite meals was blackened salmon with angel hair pasta. A man who could switch in the kitchen had most of my heart already.

"Dance with me, Nita." He reached for my hand. No one had called me Nita in years. Softly resting my hand in his, he pulled me close and we moved effortlessly to the sound of Coltrane's horn.

There was something different about the way he held me. Dumas did not hold me just as dance partner. He was a man holding his woman. I had a sensual awakening as his manhood slowly hardened against my body. His deep, lustful gaze told me that this evening held a promise of something more. I felt heat stir in my cheeks as his face moved closer to mine. I closed my eyes and anticipated the feel of Dumas' firm lips against mine. He trailed a series of light, feathery kisses over my cheeks and neck before his tongue moved between my lips. Lord, it had been awhile since I'd had the wonderful taste of a man on my lips. I knew that I should have stopped him, but it felt wickedly good. He sensed my hesitation.

"Nita, do you want to go?"

"No."

"Are you sure? Because, if you stay, we are going to make love."

"I know."

He smiled and planted a soft kiss on my forehead then took my hand in his and led me upstairs to his bedroom.

Fear paralyzed me. Reese had been my only lover and after thirty-eight years, I felt like a virgin again. Nervous and unsure.

He removed his shirt and the desire to run my fingers through the thin silver hair on his hard chest zipped through me like electricity. After he slowly undressed me, we stood naked together. The feel of my flesh against his made me oblivious to anything else. My fears were replaced by emotions that were more urgent. A hot ache grew inside of me.

Dumas stood motionless before taking the first step toward the massive bed in the center of the room, where he gently laid me on the silk duvet. There, he flicked his tongue gently across my tight nipples. My blood pounded and the desire to give and take pleasure was keen. I ran my tongue down the side of his neck, and his immediate response to my touch gave me a sense of power. He was as vulnerable as I was.

I sighed heavily as he sensuously mounted me and nudged my legs apart with his knee. I spread my legs and welcomed him into my warm, moist heat. He sank into me slowly, inch by hard, delicious inch. We sighed in unison as he filled me completely. My body was on fire.

The downward thrust of his hips was purposeful and I met each of them with a steady upward movement of my own.

"Oh, Dumas," I moaned, as I guided his ass with my hands.

"Come with me, baby," he urged in a voice that was rough with passion. "Let go."

Our rhythmic movements soon sent us over the edge as a wave of orgasm swept over us. Our soulful cries of ecstasy filled the room. We fell asleep in each other's tired yet satisfied arms.

The next month, Dumas and I celebrated our love in a small, simple ceremony on a beautiful beach in Jamaica. While exchanging our vows, I realized that some people are blessed enough to have one great love in their life. Sadly, most people search endlessly and never find their great love. I have been blessed twice: once, with Reese and now, Dumas.

I look forward to dancing through the rest of our lives together.

SIMONE'S SONG

When my brother, Craig, invited me to another one of his annual summer cookouts, I was more than a little hesitant about going. I love Craig madly, but his parties were always so one-dimensional. It was the same boring people, eating the same boring hot dogs and hamburgers and listening to the same boring music. Everyone always talked about things like how much money was raised at the last church bake sale or which football teams were bowl contenders this season or who was the best dog groomer in town. The jokes his neighbors told were never funny unless I'd smoked a joint before I left home. But, of course, Craig was my brother and I couldn't let him down. I always felt obligated to go. Besides, this time he'd gone to the trouble of inviting someone new. Someone that he thought I should meet. Even though he and his wife, Carla, always nagged me about falling in love and settling down into the life of mundane suburbia, neither of them had ever taken enough interest to introduce me to anyone. Craig insisted that he knew my type and I was more than a little curious to know if he really did.

So, I got dressed in my finest summer casuals, put the top down on my new BMW and headed over to the barbecue. When I arrived, I was pleasantly surprised by what I saw. Craig had hired valets to park the cars. The guests were definitely cut from a different cloth than the usual Stepford-like crowd. Instead of an Al Green cassette playing on the tired old boom box that Craig has owned since the original Bush was in the White House, there was an awesome live band. Wow, I thought. My big brother had truly gone all out for the first time in his life. This party was not one-dimensional. I could actually picture myself having a good time.

"Why are you standing there with your mouth open?" Craig asked, as he and Carla walked over to where I was standing. They were such a cute couple. After seven years of marriage, they still walked together, hand in hand and hung on each other's every word.

"Because I'm surprised that your fiscally responsible ass has spent money on something other than stock options and Ralph Lauren neckties," I answered.

We both laughed and embraced. Craig looked good. The afternoon sun beamed on his ebony baldness and made him appear almost angelic. Even though Craig and I lived in the same city and talked almost daily, it had been months since we'd seen each other. When we hugged, I could tell that there was a little less of him to hold on to than usual.

"You're not trying to get all fine on me now, are you?" I asked, jokingly.

"No. Just healthy. Carla's been on me to lose some weight and she's right. You know, growing up on Nana's fried chicken and macaroni and cheese put a lot of weight on a brother over the years and none of us are getting any younger."

Now that was the truth. Craig and I were raised by Nana after our mom died of cancer when we were kids. Nana was always cooking something sweet or greasy and it was always good. I swear, she never paid any attention to anything NIH or anybody else had to say about nutrition. Nana actually considered a diet to be one of the seven deadly sins. Butter, lard and more butter were the staples of our diet. We weren't rich but we never had a hungry day in our lives. Nana's remedy for everything was good southern cooking.

I was happy to know that Carla was taking such good care of my big brother. Maybe one day, I'll make the same lifestyle decision. But not today.

"So, where's this mystery person that you are dying for me to meet?" I eagerly looked around Craig's newly landscaped backyard.

"Slow your roll. We'll get to that in a minute. First, take some time and chill. Have a glass of wine and look around for a bit."

"What are you up to?"

"Just be patient," Craig said, as he and Carla left to greet some guests who had just arrived.

I was impressed. This was really an upscale gig complete with a personal chef throwing down on the huge grill and waiters to supply endless glasses of wine. The band was jamming some seriously smooth jazz. The lawn looked so luxurious. I decided to take off my sandals and let the soft blades of Bermuda grass tickle my freshly pedicured toes. Since I really didn't know any of the guests, I meandered along until I found a spot near the sparkling new pool to sit and relax with a glass of Chardonnay.

"Enjoying yourself?" I heard Craig ask from behind me.

"This is awesome, big brother. I see that Carla's suburban bourgeoisness has finally rubbed off on you."

"Whatever," he said, as he smiled and rolled his eyes.

Craig sat down on the chaise next to mine and we caught up on what was going on in each other's lives. He decided to break away from the engineering firm that he'd worked for since graduating from Morehouse to start his own firm. That's why he wanted to have this little soiree. He wanted to romance a few potential clients. Carla was pregnant again but they weren't ready to tell everyone just yet because of Carla's long history of miscarriages. I couldn't believe that in seven months, I could have a little niece or nephew to spoil absolutely rotten. Craig congratulated me on my recent promotion from field reporter to co-anchor of the local evening news.

As I was about to tell Craig that I would be closing escrow on a new condo in a few days, I was captivated by the sound of the band and by the beautiful voice that was now leading it.

It was soft and sexy. So was the creature that possessed it. She was dressed in a white gauzy sundress that hung slightly off one shoulder and nonchalantly blew in the late summer breeze. Her sandy brown hair was bone straight, barely touching the small of her tall slender back. The sun setting behind her gave her flawless golden skin a natural glow. She looked like Christmas morning. Never in my life, have I heard Love Ballad sung so sweet and soulful. I knew that I would have kicked my own ass later if I didn't meet her.

"Are you all right?" Craig asked, as he waved his hand in front of my face.

"What?" I tried to recover my breath that Simone stole from me.

"You were in another world. I guess I don't have to ask what or who took you there, huh," Craig laughed.

"Do you know her?"

"This is my party, you know. Come on, I'll introduce you."

I was glad I had not eaten yet because there were butterflies putting on a major trapeze show in my stomach. It seemed as if my feet were moving but my body wasn't. Craig and I stood at the edge of the stage until the song was finished before he beckoned her down to where we were.

"Great party, Craig," she said as she gave him a big hug.

"I want you to meet an adoring fan. Simone, this is my little sister, Phoebe."

I hoped that when I opened my mouth to speak, I wouldn't sound like a blubbering idiot.

"Phoebe, this is Simone. The person I wanted you to meet," Craig said, smiling slyly.

How did he know? I never told him that I was a lesbian. I talked to him about my relationships but only in general. Never any specifics. How did he know? I looked at him with total confusion.

"I told you I knew your type," he whispered in my ear as he walked away. I was stunned.

"Hello, Phoebe. I think Craig has wanted us to meet for a long time," Simone said.

"Really," I said, still amazed.

"You are his second favorite subject, next to Carla. He's very proud of you."

I stood there for a minute and gazed into her dark grayish blue eyes that twinkled like a thousand stars when she smiled. This sister was even more gorgeous up close. She smelled of sweet honey and I was drawn to her like a bee. I eagerly accepted her invitation to sit and talk during her break.

"I haven't had a bite to eat all day. Do you want something?" Simone asked.

She beckoned one of the waiters over for appetizers but I couldn't eat a bite. That was not easy for a fabulously thick southern girl like me to do. I just watched her, mesmerized. Simone worked as an intern at Craig's old firm and sung with the band for extra cash to help with law school. She was an only child, born and raised here in Atlanta. I could have listened to her talk all night. I could tell that Simone was just as beautiful inside as she was outside. She possessed a quiet confidence that was wickedly intoxicating. Soon, it was time for her to return to the stage to finish the set. When she sang, Simone's voice was like voodoo and I was completely under her spell. Every word of every song she sang took me to another place in time. I closed my eyes and listened as the summer breeze whispered her name in my ear.

"So, what do you think?" Craig asked.

"How did you know?"

"Know what? That you are a lesbian?"

"Yeah."

"I've always known. Shit, I think I knew before you did."

I never formally came out, if there is such a thing. I just lived my life the way I saw fit. No explanations. No excuses. I dated a few guys, in high school, but nothing ever came of those relationships. I just blew them off as being immature boys. I even had sex with a man once and it was like watching paint dry. Uneventful and unfulfilling. But the first time I made love with a woman, it was a spiritual awakening. The mountains roared, the sky bled and the sun came out at night. She kissed me and touched me in a way that was soft and nurturing. Sensual. It was unlike anything I'd experienced before. I immediately knew that this was how I wanted to be loved. I was a freshman in college when I had my first experience.

I was in my professor's office discussing supply side economics when she asked if I would have dinner with her. Convinced that dinner with my economics professor would be a good way to boost my less than mediocre grade, I accepted. All evening, she stroked the back of my hand and stared into my eyes when she talked. It seemed as if she was searching for something. At first, I thought that maybe she was just one of those people who liked touching others while they talked or that maybe she and Jack Daniels had become a little too friendly over the course of the evening. After dinner, she drove me back to my dorm, and asked, what I thought was the oddest question.

"You want to fuck me, don't you?"

"What?" I asked, surprised.

"I think you heard me."

"What kind of question is that? What do you mean?"

She leaned in closer. So close that I could smell the mix of whiskey and risotto on her breath. "Don't bullshit me, okay. You know what I mean. Do you want to fuck me? It is not a difficult question," she whispered.

I didn't know what to say or do. I just sat there, frozen.

Amused by my obvious inexperience, she gently covered my open lips with hers. Instantly, I knew that the answer to her question was yes. I became wet at the mere thought of her touching me. She fucked me in the backseat of her Jag and rocked my entire world. We were lovers for a couple of semesters. Our affair was over once her husband came home and caught his wife's head between my legs.

Simone came over to me after the party and asked if we could get together again, soon. I told her that I would like that. For the next few weeks, we talked on the phone for hours on end, chitchatting about everything, from the war in Iraq to what was happening on The Young and the Restless. I would sometimes accompany her to a gig or two on weekends. It seemed as if we were inseparable. She would come over to my place after work and I would cook some fabulous meals for her. I would joke about how skinny she was.

"Simone, I need to put some meat on your bones before your legs sue you for non-support."

We were having fun getting to know each other. Falling in love with Simone was a beautiful way to pass the lazy days of summer.

One night, I came home from work and found a note taped to my front door that read:

Phoebe,

Tonight is going to be very special for both of us. I want you to relax and let me take care of you.

I love you,

Simone

P.S. Follow the rose petals.

Opening the door, I was almost brought to tears by the sensuous atmosphere Simone had created. Candles illuminated every corner of my sparsely decorated living room. I could hear Luther Vandross serenading softly in the background as a trail of white rose petals led me down the hallway toward the bedroom. I couldn't wait to see what else Simone had in store for me.

Breathtaking, an endless canopy of white silk hung from the ceiling over my mahogany bed, as white rose petals covered the soft ivory sheets. Simone definitely knew how to set the stage for love. I wandered into the bathroom and there she was, sitting on the edge of my claw foot bathtub that was filled with bubbles and surrounded by even more roses and candles and roses. She wore a bathrobe that was opened slightly; allowing me to sneak a peek at the silhouette of her perfectly shaped breast.

I closed my eyes and inhaled the sexy scent of night blooming jasmine and vanilla. When I opened them, Simone was standing in front of me.

"Do you like?" she whispered.

I smiled and kissed her deeply, letting the dance of my tongue with hers show my approval.

She took a sip of wine and then dropped her robe to the floor, revealing her beautiful nakedness. Her slender form was exquisite. I couldn't take my eyes off her. She slowly unbuttoned my blouse. At that moment, I realized that this was going to be our first time making love. Simone had not seen me in all my glory and I became a bit anxious. I wondered how she would feel once she saw my big ass completely uncovered. Would she still want me? She sensed my apparent hesitation.

"It's okay," she said, as she softly kissed my neck.

She continued to undress me urgently. It was as if she couldn't wait to see what I'd been hiding all these weeks. She removed the barrette that held back my thick dreads and allowed them to fall freely onto my round, chocolate shoulders. And there I was, naked as a jaybird. Simone stood back and surveyed me from head to toe. Then, she smiled and nodded.

"Do you know how beautiful you are to me right now?" she asked.

"You make me feel beautiful."

"Baby, you don't need me for that," she said, as she lovingly stroked my cheek.

We held each other for a while, enjoying the heat generated by our love. Our bodies melted into each other, becoming one.

"I've been thinking about making love to you from the moment we met," Simone said.

Then, she took my hand and led me into the warm bath. We sat facing as Simone slowly bathed me. She had a way of looking into my eyes that made words seem unnecessary. I was completely aroused by her loving caress. She kissed my hard nipples, gently yet passionately. When Simone slid her fingers into my abyss, I gasped with pleasure. It had been almost a year since anyone had touched my core and it felt painfully good. I laid my head back, grabbed both sides of the tub and held on for dear life. I danced to Simone's music as she rhythmically finger fucked me with one hand and stroked my swollen clit with the other. I came so hard and so fast, that, for a moment, I couldn't catch my breath. When I came back to earth, I saw Simone licking her fingers.

"Um, sweet," she moaned.

After a bit more tub play, we took our little party to the bed. The cool air blowing from the ceiling fan on my half-wet body made my nipples even harder. The growing anticipation of showering Simone's beautiful body with pleasure made my heart pound like a drum. Simone lay on her back as I leaned over and kissed her. She allowed my tongue to explore every inch of her hot mouth. Her deep moans of ecstasy told me that I had found her sweet spot as I gently kissed her slender neck.

"Is that it, baby?" I whispered.

"Oh yeah," she replied, breathlessly.

Wanting to please her more, I continued to touch and caress her damp skin. Her nipples stood at attention like soldiers eagerly awaiting my tongue's arrival as I made slow, deliberate circles around them. I finally took one into my mouth. Simone caressed the back of my neck, breathing harder. Her glistening body writhed wildly on the bed, begging for more. I was entranced by the sweet fragrance that lingered on Simone's burning flesh. I eagerly continued my maiden voyage to her naval and then to her soft clit. My tongue moved effortlessly between her delicate folds, she bucked like a beautiful stallion. The taste of her succulent nectar drove me insane as I fed the craving that grew inside of her wet pussy. Her entire body erupted like a volcano as she pushed my face deeper. I kissed my way up Simone's trembling body just as I had kissed my way down, allowing my tongue to linger on her lips, letting her taste her own sweetness.

"I'm not done with you," she said.

Simone reached into the nightstand and pulled out a beautifully wrapped rectangular box, along with a red silk scarf.

"Put this on," she instructed, giggling like an anxious little girl who was waiting for Santa.

"What?"

"Just do it for me. I promise you'll like it."

I did as I was told. I wrapped the scarf around my eyes and laid on my back. Hovering over me, Simone kissed me intensely before a burning hardness slid inside of me, striking my core like a wildfire, completely consuming me. As I reached for the scarf, Simone grabbed both my hands and pulled my arms out to my side and entwined her fingers with mine

"No peeking."

My entire body was an inferno as Simone made love to me. I met each of her artistic strokes with my own.

"Simone," I whined, repeatedly.

"Ssssss, it feels good to me too, baby."

"Ooh shit."

"Ssssss, I'm writing my name all over your pussy."

The sound of our bodies rhythmically loving each other was beautifully deafening.

My burning pussy enjoyed the song Simone's gentle thrusts were making it sing. We exploded at the same time; whimpering and cussing as sweeping waves of orgasm overtook us both.

When I removed the scarf, I saw Simone's weapon of mass seduction was still strapped on. Hard and ready for more action. Of course, I didn't know if I could take any more.

"You are something else, girl," I said, as I lovingly stroked Simone's back.

"I have a lot more surprises planned for you this evening, baby. Just wait."

"No need to rush, Simone. We have a lifetime together."

SURRENDER

I took a trip with my husband several weeks ago, that turned out to be a life altering experience. We would have never imagined that spending intense one on one time together would drastically change our relationship forever. It changed the way we looked at the entire world and the way we saw each other, and our marriage.

Married for seven years, Ahmad and I met during our junior year at Georgetown. I'd admired his phenomenal skills on the basketball court for a while before we were formally introduced by one of my sorors after a game. It was love at first sight for Ahmad. He says that he knew we were meant for each other from the moment he held my hand and looked into my eyes. Destiny is what he called it. Cupid's proverbial arrow didn't hit me in the ass until a few months later. Ahmad was definitely a delicious treat for my eyes. He was a beautifully sculpted ballplayer with mile long legs and a rock hard ass. Long, thick lashes hovered sleepily above his dark thoughtful eyes and he had dimples that were deep enough to swim in. But, I needed to know what the brother was truly made of inside. I needed to see and feel the soul of the man. I was pleased to discover that his game on and off the court was just as smooth, and as rich, as his espresso skin.

After a year of dating, we were married soon after graduation. He went straight to law school while I worked as a high school history teacher. After our first child was born, I quit my job to stay at home and take care of my family. The first few years of our marriage were not easy because of Ahmad's intense love affair with his work. He was always working, even when he was at home. His drive to be an exceptional attorney at the absolute exclusion of everything else was a source of many fights. Ahmad's idea of compromise was for me to adjust my expectations. I was drowning in an ocean of tedium.

"I can't continue to maintain the standard of living that you've become so accustomed to. Do you think that we can live in this big house and drive a new Lexus every other year if I don't work, and work hard?"

I understood that as a Black man, Ahmad felt as if he had something to prove.

However, I also needed, and missed, my husband. My lover.

After years of sacrifice, Ahmad became one of the most successful labor attorneys in the state and the first African American partner in his law firm. To the naked eye, our life together appeared perfect.

Because Ahmad worked so hard, to make sure that we had all the material luxuries we could ever want, sometimes he would not get home until nine or ten at night. Our sex life suffered. Tired and worn out from taking care of the house and chasing the girls all day, most times I was already asleep by the time he climbed into bed. There was never enough time to make love, really. All we seemed to have time for were quickies on the couch, in Ahmad's home office, during a rare break from his work. No more than five or ten minutes. On occasions, when we would have more time, Ahmad wanted us to be more adventurous and try different positions or use sex toys. This made me uncomfortable. If I'd said no, an argument would be inevitable.

"I don't understand you, Nikki! What's wrong with a man wanting to make love to his wife in a position other than missionary?"

Ahmad was right. I understood his frustration. In my heart, I knew there was nothing wrong with any of the things that he wanted us to do. But, in my mind, I found it hard to get pass all of the hang-ups I had when it came to sex.

Anything other than the missionary position was too risqué. I felt it cheapen our lovemaking to have my husband behind me instead of on top. Every time he would attempt to go down on me, I would freeze. All I would hear was the sound of my prim and proper mother's voice in my ear, declaring that oral sex was the work of the devil.

Ahmad was my first everything; my first boyfriend and my first lover. My father was a strict minister who never allowed me to date as a teenager. When I was in high school, I made the mistake of giving a guy my phone number and my father had a fit.

"You are not to have boys call or come by to see you. Do you hear me? They just want one thing and once they get it, you'll be left with nothing but regret and a screaming bastard to raise. I will not allow that kind of shame on my house or my church," he yelled.

My mother was not as loud; however, the message was basically the same. "Save yourself. Sex is for your husband's pleasure. You won't enjoy it. Just lie there and bare it until he is done. It's your duty," my mother had said.

Orgasm? No. I'd never allowed myself to let go and truly enjoy the total lovemaking experience. I enjoyed the feeling of having Ahmad inside of me and I waited for the day when he would make my toes curl and my hair stand straight up on my head, but it never happened. Through it all, Ahmad remained somewhat patient. I knew he wanted more from me but would take whatever I could give. I would see the frustration in his eyes when I would say no to him and I could hear it in his voice when he'd asked why.

"You need to get your mama and daddy out of our bedroom so that we can do our thing," Ahmad pleaded.

I so wanted things to be different in our bedroom. My girlfriends even gave me advice on how to spice things up but I was afraid that some of their suggestions would take me too far away from my comfort zone. One suggested that I take a pole dancing class and put on a strip show for Ahmad. The other believed that I should let him watch me pleasure myself with a vibrator. There was no way that either of these ideas would work unless I could learn to relax, relate and release with my husband.

Last month, someone from Ahmad's office invited us to spend the weekend at his house in the country. We jumped at the chance to go and spend some quality time alone with each other. We usually declined any offers to spend time away from our girls, but Ahmad and I hadn't been away alone together since our honeymoon and were in need of a little rest and relaxation. It was time to be husband and wife. Man and woman. Not Daddy and Mommy. I thought that maybe a change in venue would be the inspiration I'd hoped for. So, we packed our bags, dropped our children off at my parents' house and set off for the country.

I loved everything about the Pennsylvania countryside especially during the fall. There was something magical about the red and golden hues of fallen leaves and the sound of them crunching under my feet; the chilly crispness of the fresh air and the smells of hot apple cider and sweet potato pie. I looked over at my gorgeous husband in his black turtleneck sweater and tight blue jeans, commanding the steering wheel of his white Hummer and became excited about reconnecting with him. I exhaled and felt instant calm. After about three hours of driving, Ahmad and I thought our GPS system was off track or that there was a mix up with address and we were lost. There were no houses on the highway and we couldn't recall seeing any other cars on the road for miles. Surrounded by thick woods and the occasional deer jetting across the narrow rural road, I remembered the news reporting stories of people getting lost and becoming the victims of foul play or some wild animal's mid-afternoon snack.

"This is where we are supposed to turn?" Ahmad asked. He tried not to sound nervous. But I knew he was.

After turning onto another seemingly deserted road, I tried to convince Ahmad to turn around and go back home. Then, all of a sudden, a huge house seemed to appear out of nowhere.

This was not just any house. It was nothing short of a majestic mansion. The ivy-covered stoned walls and tall timeworn columns gave the house the appearance of a medieval castle. I could have sworn that I even saw a bat fly out of the belfry.

"Are you sure this is the place?" I asked.

"Yeah."

Neither of us wanted to be the first to get out of the car. We sat and stared at the massive iron and glass front door.

Finally, Ahmad got out. "Come on."

A short, round-faced man wearing an old black tuxedo, which made him look more like an undertaker than a butler, greeted us at the door. "Mr. and Mrs. Jacobs?"

We both nodded, hesitantly.

"We've been eagerly expecting you. This way, please."

He took our bags and escorted Ahmad and I through the excessively grand marble foyer to our enormous suite.

When Ahmad asked about our hosts, the man just shrugged his tired shoulders and grunted, "Later."

The suite to which we were assigned was not at all what I'd imagined. I had never seen anything so luxurious in my life. Not even on the Home and Garden channel. There were fresh Casablanca lilies arranged in a beautiful crystal vase that commanded the top of an antique Biedermeier chest. The massive king-sized canopy bed was draped with ivory silk panels and dressed in gorgeous linen that had already been turned down for us, with European chocolates on each pillow. In a sterling silver ice bucket, on the stunning round mahogany dining table, was a chilled bottle of expensive champagne. A trail of white rose petals led to the bathroom that was an oasis of white, fluffy towels and exotic scented candles. Everything was designed for lovers. This was definitely the way to do the whole romance thing and I couldn't wait to get started.

Just as my husband and I were about to share our first kiss of the weekend, the telephone rang. When I answered, a man's voice on the other end instructed me to turn on the speakerphone so that Ahmad could hear him as well. He said our hosts requested our presence in the library. He also said that we were to shower and put on the long, plush white bathrobes that were hanging behind the door of the bathroom, before we came downstairs. Then, there was a dial tone.

Ahmad and I were confused by the instructions but we did as we were told. For the first time, we showered together and lovingly washed each other. I was amazed by how turned on I became with Ahmad's slippery hands caressing my entire body. It felt so damned good! We resisted the temptation to have a quick tryst in the shower and decided to wait until we could take our time together later. Both of us hoped that this little meet and greet wouldn't take too long because we wanted to come back to the room and get our fuck on.

When we arrived in the library, we were surprised to realize that we were not the only people invited to the estate for the weekend. There were about four other couples there as well.

Everyone was stunned with the presence of everyone else. We all spent a few minutes starring suspiciously at each other. Then, an older couple appeared from behind frosted French doors at the far corner of the room. My husband whispered to me that the man was Percy H. Willoughby, V., the founding partner of his law firm. The woman was a tall, slender sister with long flowing silver dreadlocks. He was shorter, plumper, balder and whiter. They were both wearing white bathrobes as well. The couple slowly circled us, sized up each couple and exchanged sly smiles with each other. I didn't know what to expect and was about to quickly exit stage right.

After giving everyone the once over, the older woman spoke while the man stood beside her with his stubby arms folded, with a Cuban cigar nonchalantly dangling from his mouth.

"Hello, I am the Madam of the house and my husband and I want to welcome you to our home. You all are friends or associates of ours and have been invited here to share a very special weekend with us. You and your lover have been carefully selected to spend a time with us that will prove to be both relaxing and exhilarating. You are here because your lover has become common. You no longer have that burning desire that you once had for each other. We have brought you here to help you find that which has been lost. You will discover things about yourselves that you never knew and remember those things that have been long forgotten.

"You will be turned on like never before. We will make sure of that. You will be allowed to do whatever makes you and your lover feel good. No one will be criticized or judged by what they do here. What happens here this weekend will not be shared with anyone, at anytime, anywhere. The butler has confidentiality agreements for you to sign to insure your privacy and discretion. We encourage you to touch, kiss, watch and do what comes naturally. You will explore each other while discovering yourselves. There are only two rules you must follow for our first exercise: One, you cannot talk. You may communicate only by touch. Two, you will be blindfolded. No one will know with whom they are with. We've planned this to be a very sensual weekend for you all. If you wish not to participate in what I have just explained to you, you and your lover may leave. No questions or judgments. I will give you a few moments to talk it over with your lover and then we'll begin."

After her speech, the woman and the old man left the room.

At first, everyone was quiet. Then, I could hear the monotone voices asking each other, "What do you think?"

Ahmad and I were almost dumbstruck with awe. I asked him if he had any idea that this was going to be a wild orgy and he assured me that he didn't. He said that no one told him that his boss was into this kind of freaky shit. Ahmad said the Percy H. Willoughby, V he knew appeared to be the most straight-laced Republican he had ever met in his life. I was not quite sure what to think but I must admit that a part of me was a bit intrigued. I had read about places like this before but I never dreamed I would ever find myself as a part one. This was definitely different. Ahmad said he would leave if I wanted to but I could tell that he was more than a little curious, too. We looked at each other and said what the hell. We agreed to stay and play. We both hoped that this weekend would not end up as an episode of HBO's Real Sex. Surprisingly, all of the couples remained. All of us had the look of a deer stuck in headlights. We had no idea of what we were about to get into. After the Madam returned, we all signed the confidentiality agreements and were asked not to speak once we had signed on the dotted line. The butler blindfolded each of us and the games began.

Once blindfolded, my other senses were quickly awakened. The sexy scent of lavender, sandalwood and vanilla wandered to my nose. It was sensuously intoxicating. I heard classical piano playing softly in the background. We all knew our original partners were sitting on the floor directly across from us, and were told to begin with them. Ahmad immediately started doing all the things he knew I loved but had not done in a very long time. He clumsily reached for my breasts and once found, he suckled them—one then the other—before he nursed like a baby. Becoming extremely moist and, of course, wanting more, Ahmad obviously sensed my growing excitement as I reached for his hand and directed it to my hot pussy. He played a tune on my clit with his fingers before sliding them inside my wetness, causing me to tremble and gyrate like a drunken jackrabbit. I was a bit embarrassed at first, but then I realized that no one could see us. I surrendered to the ecstasy that encircled me and did what came naturally. This new freedom made my juices run uncontrollably rampant. I couldn't keep my hands off of Ahmad either. I grabbed his swollen dick and stroked it slowly and steadily, with precision. Ahmad moaned deeply as I ran my index finger down the center of his balls to the crack of his ass and gently inserted it. He squealed like a little bitch at first but enjoyed the sensation of my finger moving slowly in and out. We both were dripping wet with desire. It seemed as if the blindfolds had somehow heightened our senses and made everything that we were doing to each other appear fresh and new. I felt the heat of everyone else in the room as well as our own. Their beastly moans and breathless sighs of pleasure only turned me on even more. I wanted Ahmad inside of me. I wanted him to fill me up, completely, bringing me to my knees with a mind-blowing orgasm, again and again.

Just as my husband and I were about to begin to dance the 69, someone took my hand and led me away from Ahmad and to a new partner. My new lover and I just stood and held hands for a minute like two little kids that were being forced to play nice on the playground. I felt two warm hands touch my face and then my new lover's first kiss. Our tongues danced together in a symphony of lust with each other. My new lover's tongue was large and thick and explored my mouth in ways my husband never had, touching and tasting everything inside. I felt as though I was having an out of body experience. I wondered who and what Ahmad was doing. We both knew that we would never tolerate infidelity from each other and I questioned whether or not this weekend would compromise that. My thoughts of Ahmad were quickly brought to a screeching halt when my new lover started to descend to my lower zip code.

Oh my goodness!!! I was overcome by what seemed like a thousand tiny flashes of lightening striking the walls of my wet pussy. The sound of my new lover slurping my juices drove me insane. Boy, was my mother wrong about oral sex, I thought. Probably because she'd never had it. I was quickly taken aback by the touch of another tongue on my right nipple. I didn't know what to think but I knew exactly how to feel; absolutely fabulous! Everything seemed to be happening so fast that my head was spinning as if I had just drunk a whole pitcher of Long Island Iced Tea. For the first time in my life, I wasn't thinking about my actions or what other people were going to think of them. I was letting go and reacting to the absolute maddening pleasure I was receiving. My nipples were so hard; they felt as if they were going to explode into a million pieces. I bucked and moaned, and whimpered, as my body enjoyed intensely marvelous activity. The waves of my first orgasm rushed like a tsunami, overtaking me and completely wiped out any and all inhibitions.

I wanted to return the pleasure to both these savage creatures. I reached over to find the face of my nipple sucker and kissed him deeply and passionately.

Even though we had been instructed not to speak, I whispered my intentions for him in his ear. I reached down, felt his massive, throbbing dick and knew immediately that I wanted to ride this stallion into the next lifetime. I could not let this piece of solid granite go to waste. I also couldn't leave out the talented pussy eater either. So, I reached over to find the face that had been skillfully buried so deeply in my rainforest and my hand landed on a breast. I gasped with confusion and wanted to remove my blindfold. The Madam of the manor must have been watching us because the moment I reached for my blindfold, she announced, "Remember, peeking is against the rules."

I took a deep breath and reached again. The breast was still there. I must admit, I had always wondered about the mystique of making love to a woman. It was one of those secret fantasies that many women have but few will openly acknowledge, while sober, and one I never thought I would get the chance to experience.

I threw caution to the wind and I kissed her as deeply as I had my other lover and promised with each lick inside her soft cheeks that I would rock her world.

Beginning our rhythmic dance, I slowly mounted my male lover making sure I savored each pulsating inch of his huge muscle. With each thrust, he was deeper and deeper inside my wet orb. It was so hard to keep quiet while I was being fucked into oblivion. My female lover made sure she was not left out. She stood in front of me and pushed my face into her waiting, wet cunt. The scent of her freshly bathed hair coupled with the sweet aura of her excitement was one not to be forgotten. My first taste of a woman drove me wild. She wiggled like a playful puppy as she held my head tightly with both hands as if she would snap my neck if I stopped. I licked her soft folds and then searched for her rosebud. I darted my tongue playfully in and out of her wet hole and felt her knees weaken, while keeping a steady, slow pace with my buck wild stallion. With each movement, his pole inched deeper inside of me and I felt myself about to lose total control! I suspected my female lover was about to explode and leave her honey all over my face as well. The three of us came in unison and it seemed as if the earth below would open up and swallow us whole. We all lay exhausted and satisfied with our performances. I lay in the arms of my female lover and we stroked each other to sleep.

I was awakened when someone removed my blindfold. I immediately looked around to find my husband. Ahmad was over between two women, looking just as satisfied. Our eyes locked and it seemed we were thinking the same thought.

What in the hell have we done?

We were told to return to our suites and make love to our own lovers. Our lovemaking should now be more fulfilling and the ecstasy heightened, according to the Madam. We should feel uninhibited and should not hold back.

When Ahmad and I returned to our room, we talked openly about what had just occurred. I expressed disappointment over the fact that Ahmad was not the person to give me my first orgasm. It seemed as if I had somehow betrayed him. He listened and understood why I felt the way I did.

"I'm just glad that you've had that experience, Nikki. The person who gave the orgasm to you had you for that moment. I have you forever."

We both felt somehow liberated, yet a little confused. I still felt as if something was missing. And it was. I had not made passionate love to my husband. I wanted him in every possible way. Even though I enjoyed having sex with the others, there were things that only Ahmad could give me. Only he could give me love and intimacy. Only he knew where my spot was. He seemed to have read my mind because he held me for a while before touching me in all the right places. Each touch and kiss was gentle and purposeful. In the shower, we gazed into each other's eyes as we touched and lovingly explored each other's wet bodies.

"I want to taste you," Ahmad said, as he started to go down on me.

I lie on the bed; ready to be taken wherever my husband wanted to go.

Ahmad started by kissing his way down my treasure trail to his favorite new vacation spot where my legs opened automatically, like the doors to the Ritz-Carlton, to greet his arrival. He licked and nibbled at my clit. He ate me like I was his last meal before going to the gas chamber. He slid his slender tongue inside of me and tongue-fucked me until I could no longer close my mouth nor remember my name. He had never done this to me before and I wondered if I'd missed out on this fabulous feeling for years or if it was a new trick he had picked up during one of his earlier rendezvous. Wherever he learned it, it was making me feel so good. I closed my eyes and exhaled. I surrendered completely to the feeling of loving my husband and letting him love me. I came so hard that my pussy sung his name aloud. When he kissed me, I could taste my sweet nectar on his lips.

"I want you to fuck me from behind," I said.

Ahmad was stunned because this was a position that he always wanted to try with me but one I had serious hang-ups about. But, today seemed to be the perfect day for trying new things.

"Are you sure?" He was holding his hard dick that appeared to get harder in anticipation of a new adventure.

I stood up, leaned over the bed and spread my legs wide, signaling my unwavering desire. He came over, kissed the nape of my neck before running his tongue down my back, giving me goose bumps.

He teased my wet opening with the tip of his hot rod before sliding it in ever so gently. I was surprised at how good it felt. I was already creaming and this was just the beginning! My entire body shook like a leaf on a tree as Ahmad tightly held my waist and pumped my juicy tunnel.

"I've been waiting to fuck you all day," he whispered, breathlessly.

With each thrust, Ahmad went deeper and deeper into me until I didn't know where he began and I ended. We were completely absorbed by each other. I stroked my clit with my soaked fingers. This almost drove me to insanity. As our excitement grew, so did our rhythm. I couldn't remember Ahmad's dick ever being so big and hard. It felt as if he was going to pound the bottom right out of me. I made sure to meet each of his hard thrusts with my own. Ahmad grabbed my hands and pulled my arms out to the side and continued fucking me until he came, growling like a Doberman and pumping all of his love into me. I could feel myself on the edge of another orgasm so I locked my pussy muscles around his still throbbing dick and dared him to pull out. I continued to slap my ass against him until I, too, oozed all over him. We wore each other's satisfaction like a badge of honor.

Each time we made love, or fucked each other, that weekend, it was just as exciting.

The rest of the weekend proved as interesting as the first day. We tried all types of new things with all types of new people and with each other.

After returning home, we both vowed never to mention that weekend again, not even to each other. Those few days made a difference in our relationship. Ahmad and I now take the time to give and receive pleasure in one form or another every night. Ahmad still sometimes works long hard hours but we make sure to play even harder.

SWEET HOME, ALABAMA

Summertime. When, as the song goes, the living is easy. Yeah, right. Had the writer of those beautiful and carefree lyrics ever attended one of my family's reunions, the lines of the song would have definitely included something about the bowels of hell coupled with wrist-splitting anguish. Sometimes, just being around them for any length of time makes me want to burn my eyes out with kerosene and a lit match. I love my family, especially now that I live in Philadelphia and they are far, far away in Alabama. I am thankful to God that I only have to subject myself to this kind of agony on special occasions like funerals, a few choice weddings and, of course, summer reunions.

Sweet Home, Alabama. A small sleepy town nestled in a corner of one of the poorest counties in the state. When I graduated from high school, I left Sweet Home for the first time in my life to go college at NYU, on scholarship. I wanted to get as far away from the dismal smell of rural dirt covered roads and jailed hopelessness as any plane, train or automobile could take me. I was scared shitless once I got to New York City. The flashing lights and the deafening noises took some time to get use to but my headstrong determination far outweighed all of my fears. I knew that there had to be more to life than what the one-traffic-light town of Sweet Home had to offer and I was in the right place to get it. People rarely ever moved away from Sweet Home and nobody new ever, ever came to live there. Just the same people doing the same things as they always did. Working hard and being poor. My grandparents raised me from the day I was born. I've never seen either of my parents. My mother was one of very few people who actually left Sweet Home, for a minute anyway. She was hauntingly beautiful with light caramel brown skin and long straight black hair. She sang in the church choir and was apparently pretty good at it. But, singing for the Lord obviously didn't yield the big bucks or the glamorous stardom she desperately craved.

She moved to Detroit to chase her dream of becoming the next major production off the Motown assembly line. She must have worn naiveté like perfume because she hooked up with the first no good pimp to smell her country ass as soon as she stepped off the bus. He turned her out and she returned to Sweet Home a pregnant junkie. The story goes that an hour after giving birth to me, on the back porch of her parent's shotgun house, she was gone. No one has seen or heard from her since. When I was a little girl, I would hear my grandmother praying and crying late at night for God to take care of her baby girl, wherever she may have been in the world. Granny Lou prayed for Him to bring her only child back home to the warmth and comfort of her bosom. When I was twelve, a man came to Granny's house with a yellow envelope. Her baby girl was dead. Shot through the heart when a pimp, somewhere out west, accused her of stealing from him.

"Everybody can't wait to see you, child. Especially your Papas and me. It's been five years, you know," Granny said during our last phone conversation.

Five years. To me it seemed like just last week since the last family reunion after which I swore to myself, and anyone else who would listen, that it would be the last one I would attend. I'd had enough greasy food and unemployed gold-tooth cousins to last several lifetimes. I only had one problem though. My inability to say no to Granny Lou. I knew how hard she and Papas worked to raise me, and the sacrifices they made just to educate me. Granny Lou took in laundry and sewing to make money, while Papas did odd jobs here and there. I didn't have the heart to disappoint them.

"Yes, Granny. I can't wait to see you and Papas either," I reassured.

Truth is, I was a little excited about my trip to Sweet Home this time. I hoped to get the chance to see Monica.

Monica and I were best friends as little girls. Inseparable. We ran around in the fields, chased rabbits and stole blackberries from Miss Geneva's curb market. As teenagers, we became secret lovers; we did each other's hair and watched Soul Train together. Monica was my first love. For me, the sun rose and set beautifully on her. After I went away to college, Monica stayed in Sweet Home and later married the town's most eligible bachelor, Reverend Jackson. He was much older than Monica, about fifteen years older and violently possessive. Granny Lou would tell me about Monica coming to church functions with a black eye or broken arm.

"She needs somebody to talk to, child. You two were so close and she took it hard when you left for school," Granny always said.

I'm sure Granny didn't realize just how close Monica and I really were. I never revealed the true nature of our relationship, not because I was afraid or ashamed. Granny Lou just never really seemed interested in my love life. I wrote Monica several letters while I was away in New York but they all were returned, unopened. Whenever I would come home during Christmas or Spring Break, Monica would always be too busy with church affairs or she and the Reverend would be out of town at some revival. I wanted to sit down and talk with my old friend. My best friend. My lover. I wanted to spend time with her.

Just getting to Sweet Home was an awkward adventure. I had to fly from Philly into the Birmingham airport, rent a car and drive one hundred fifty miles to Sweet Home. The only other way to get to Sweet Home was by bus and I absolutely refused to come back to this town on the bus for reasons that are too numerous to mention.

Alabama in the summertime was a different kind of hot. It was hell hot. In Philly, a cool late afternoon breeze meandered from the Delaware River and enveloped the outdoors in a romantic crispness. Some evenings, I would leave my patio doors open and enjoy the fresh air. In Alabama, it felt like the sun was literally leaning on my back like a heavy fur coat. Much to my dismay, Granny Lou did not have air conditioning and had no plans of getting one. At night, the only way to cool off was to lay butt naked on the back porch swing, while mosquitoes as big as a fat man's shoe ate me for dinner. Granny came to visit me once in Philadelphia and she complained the whole time about how cold it was. It was August and she slept in a wool sweater.

When I arrived at Granny Lou's, I just sat in driveway for a moment and enjoyed the cool air conditioning of my rented Benz. I watched the activity of my schizophrenic family members coming and going. Of course, the usual suspects were in attendance. My loud Aunt Clara and her alcoholic common law husband, Jake, never missed an opportunity to show their asses in front of the family. Jake always got drunk and pissed and/or vomited on himself and anything else in his way. Aunt Clara would then start screaming, calling him a sorry motherfucka, declaring to anyone that would listen that she was going to leave his drunk ass for real this time. Usually before the day was done, someone would catch them fucking in Granny's only bathroom or on the propane tank out behind the house. Then, there's my cousin, Sapphire, whose real name is Cleophus Wayne. Sapphire decided to come out of the closet at the last family reunion by arriving at Granny Lou's wearing his version of J Lo's infamous green dress and big hair. Cousin Frieda Mae and her nine children were always good for all kinds of painful aggravation. Uncle "Bud," well, no explanation needed.

I'd hoped to be able to sneak into the house undetected and somehow blend in until I found Granny Lou.

"Lord, have mercy. My baby is home," Granny exclaimed, halting all activity within a five-mile radius. She grabbed and held me tightly in one of her famous big mama bear hugs for what seemed like an hour. The savory smell of fresh cooked collard greens blended with her sweet Estee Lauder perfume brought back fond childhood memories of what life was like growing up in this house. After greeting everyone and hearing about how thin I had become while living in the big city, I decided to grab an apron and help out in the kitchen.

"No, child. You've been on a plane all day and you just drove all the way down from Birmingham. Bless your heart. I know you must be tired. Us old ladies got the food. You go someplace and rest. We'll call you when we fixin' to eat," my aunt Maxine directed.

I was not going to argue with her for two reasons: there's really no point, because Aunt Maxine always got her way, always, and I didn't like to cook. I decided to take a walk and look around. I waved at Papas, who was out by the smokehouse; working the pit and telling lies along with the rest of the men. The barbecue smelled wonderful. I kept walking until I reached the shallow pond that separated Granny's property from the town's sawmill. I stood there and skipped rocks like I used to do when I was a little girl. I was thankful for this place. Even though there was a lot of mayhem and foolishness going on back at the house, it felt good to be here. I always left Sweet Home with a peacefulness that was hard to come by in Philadelphia. Sweet Home was home.

I spent the rest of the day eating Granny's and Aunt Maxine's good southern home cooking and laughing at, and with, my relatives. Everyone got a good laugh at me when I cussed Monkey, Papas' blind and deaf dog for shitting on my new Jimmy Choo mules. I stayed up late and helped Granny and Aunt Maxine with the cleanup.

When I asked about Monica, Aunt Maxine just shook her head and said, "Lord, have mercy."

"It's pitiful child," Granny answered.

"What is?" I asked.

"Reverend Jackson is gonna hurt that girl real bad one of these days."

"Or kill her," Aunt Maxine chimed.

"If it's that bad, why doesn't she leave him?"

"And do what?" Aunt Maxine asked. "She ain't got no place to go. Her ma and pa both dead and buried."

I sincerely prayed that Granny and Aunt Maxine were grossly over-exaggerating the situation. They were known for doing that from time to time. Surely, Monica knew that she didn't have to stay with an abusive husband. She had to know that she had options. I needed to see Monica and talk to her myself to know what really was happening. The next day, that's just what I did.

When I walked into Solid Rock First Baptist Church, I couldn't believe my eyes. Sitting on the front row was the one person in

Sweet Home that didn't look familiar to me at all. This woman's entire body appeared to be swollen all over. Her white polyester suit didn't fit her attractively. Even though I only saw her from behind, I could tell that something was dreadfully wrong. After service, I waited for her outside. She walked slowly and carefully behind her husband as they descended the narrow brick steps and shook the hands of well-wishing and quietly sympathetic parishioners.

"Monica," I said, as they passed me on the walkway.

"That's Sister Jackson, young lady," the Reverend barked.

She turned and looked at me. Even through the netting from her hat that hung sadly over her bruised face, I saw the emptiness in her once vibrant dark eyes.

"Tracy. It's been a long time. How are you?" she asked.

She looked at me as if we were strangers.

"Yes, it has been a long time," I said as I stepped toward her in hope of a hug between old friends. Instead of meeting me halfway, she retreated behind her stubby little husband.

"Sister Tracy Woods. I have heard so much about you from your grandmother," Rev. Jackson said. "She brags about you and the work you do at the newspaper in Philadelphia. Sweet Home sure is proud of you."

He went on and on with his bullshit but I quickly tuned him out. I was too concerned about his wife. She wasn't even a shell of the person that I once knew. Monica was always the one who would tell people where to get off and how to get there whenever she felt like it. Granny was right. This was a very sad situation. Monica was about one hundred pounds heavier than I remembered and with dark circles under her puffy eyes, and several time-healed scratches and cuts on her face.

"Well, we hope to see you in church again before you go back to the big city," he said as he grabbed Monica's elbow, indicating that it was time to go.

"Monica, I hope that you and I can get together and have lunch or something before I leave," I said, hoping to see some light in her eyes.

When she opened her mouth to speak, the asshole interrupted.

"Sister Jackson stays right busy with her missionary work and such for the church. She doesn't have time for leisurely lunches."

"I was talking to Monica, Reverend," I said as I stared him hard and square in his deceitful eyes. We stood there for what seemed like a half-hour, staring each other down. Once he realized that I was not going to turn tail and run, he did what comes naturally to all reptiles. He slithered away.

"Have a blessed day, Sister Woods," he said as he walked away, pulling his mute wife behind him.

I was not going to leave Sweet Home this time without talking to Monica. I remembered reading in the church bulletin that Reverend Jackson was going to be in Biloxi for a conference next week. I decided that I would wait until then to go and see Monica. I hoped that with her interpreter out of town, she and I would finally talk. My heart ached as I approached the doublewide trailer where Monica lived. From the outside, it appeared as if no one lived there.

"Tracy, what are you doing here?" Monica asked through the chained door.

"I came to see you. May I come in?"

"My husband is out of town."

"Good, because I didn't come to see him."

"I don't–"

"Monica, it's me. I just want to know how you're doing. We haven't really talked since I left Sweet Home," I pleaded.

She hesitantly removed the chain and opened the door. Once I was inside, Monica still would not look at me directly. I sat down on the plastic-covered couch, and immediately stuck to it. The room was clean and sparsely decorated. There was no art on the dingy papered walls except for a picture of Jesus next to one of the Reverend. It was pitiful.

"May I offer you a cool drink?" Monica asked, pointing toward a pitcher of iced tea that sat on the dining table in the corner.

"Thank you. That would be great," I answered. "You know, I forget how thirsty I get whenever I'm down here. It's so hot."

Monica handed me the glass and for a brief second, our hands touched. Hers were lifeless and cold. I realized that if there was going to be any conversation between us, I would have to initiate it. So, I asked about some of the characters that she and I went to high school with. Slowly, she relaxed. I saw the light that was once in her eyes trying to shine through. She even laughed out loud, once or twice.

"You look good," she said.

"Thank you. My Pilates instructor is a bitch but she does her job."

"How are you really doing, Monica? Are you happy?" I asked, once I felt that she had let down her guard a little.

"I'm fine."

I moved closer and gently lifted her chubby chin with my hand.

"Really?"

There was a pregnant pause. Then, I saw one lonely tear roll down her dark cheek. She didn't bother catching it. Another, then another, and another followed it, until there was an uncontrollable shower of sorrowfulness. Pulling her close to me, I held my best friend. She resisted at first but quickly surrendered, lying limp in my arms, crying like a lost child.

Once Monica was able to control her sobs, she opened up like the pearly gates about everything. She explained how hurt and alone she felt when I left for college. Even though her mind understood that I was not going away forever, her heart was broken and confused. She felt that I would not be the same person when I returned home and that I would have outgrown her. She knew that I would have found someone else. Someone more sophisticated, more intellectual. Reverend Jackson had a little money and a lot of respect in Sweet Home, and he seemed to be very interested in her. After dating for a month or two, they got married. He was the first man, and the only other person besides me, that she'd known intimately. He was abusive both physically and verbally from the beginning. He didn't allow her to have any friends or any freedom. Her every move was carefully calculated by her husband. Three miscarried babies had been innocent victims of their destructive union.

"Do you want to leave this man, Monica?"

She looked at me strangely. "I can't. I have no place to go."

"There is always someplace to go but you have to want to go there. Are you ready?"

"I don't know."

"You don't have to stay here and put up with this shit, Monica. There are people who love and care for you. People who are willing to help you. You can even come back to Philly with me."

"With you? What, on earth, would I do in Philadelphia? I'm a country girl."

"Whatever you want." She laughed and shook her head.

I leaned in, kissed her cheek and then her full lips. Monica kissed me back. Hesitantly at first, but she soon gave in to the familiarness of our love. She opened her mouth, inviting me to come in, deeply. Our tongues quickly found each other, celebrating our reunion. My heart leaped and I felt that I had finally come home to everything and everyone that I loved.

"I have not made love since you left. My husband just fucks me when he wants. Most times, he doesn't even care if I'm awake," Monica whispered.

I didn't reply to her confession. While kissing the cradle of her thick collarbone, I slid my hand under her blouse and softly caressed her full breast, playfully teasing her tight nipple with my thumb.

She closed her eyes, exhaled and released the weight of the world.

"I still love you, Tracy," she said, breathlessly.

As she reclined back on the couch, I reached under her skirt and gently tugged at her panties. Gazing at me, she raised her hips and I slowly removed pulled them down around her ankles before I softly planted butterfly kisses on the inside of her thighs before descending to her swollen clit. Her hips responded rhythmically to my every motion. Her low and seductive moans, coupled with the steady hum of the window fan, made me dizzy with desire. Monica cried out when I inserted my fingers inside of her warm moistness. She came almost instantly and drenched my entire hand with the downpour of her long stored nectar. I couldn't resist the temptation to lick Monica's juices from my fingers. The sweet taste of her immediately brought back incredible memories.

"Are you crying?"

"I can't help it, Monica. I've missed you so much."

I didn't expect anything in return. Her happiness was all that mattered to me at that moment. I wanted Monica to feel me and know that I never stopped loving her.

"What do I do now?" she asked.

"It's up to you, sweetie." I walked toward the door. "I'll be driving to Birmingham on Friday. My flight to Philly leaves Saturday morning."

The next few days were quiet. Monica didn't call or come by Granny's. I didn't bother her either. I figured that she had a lot to sort through in order to make a decision that she could live with. Maybe her silence meant she already had.

Friday came and I was loading the car with all the stuff that I had accumulated in the past week. Granny Lou made sure that I had a couple of her homemade quilts and hand stitched underwear before I left. She and Papas wanted to send me back to Philadelphia with enough pound cake, fried catfish and barbecued ribs to last a lifetime but I politely talked them out of it. I gave each of them a hug and slipped five one-hundred-dollar bills into Papas overall pocket. I knew that he'd find it after I was gone.

Just as I was about to put the car into drive, I saw Monica limping hurriedly up the road. I got out ran to meet her. We embraced and kissed right there in the presence of my family and anyone else who may have been watching.

"Are you sure?" I asked as tears flowed freely down my hot sweaty face.

"All I have are the clothes on my back," she answered, trying to catch her breath.

"You have everything you'll ever need in me."

I saw Granny crying tears of joy and waving her pink lace handkerchief as Monica and I drove away.

TIRAMISU

"What do you mean he don't eat pussy," Aunt Geraldine asked, shocked.

"He insists that where he comes from, brothers don't do that," I explained.

"Shiiiiiiit, I'm glad I ain't where he's from."

My eighty-seven year old Aunt Geraldine looked utterly disgusted with the revelation of my sexual frustration with my new husband. Until now, she thought Andre hung the moon. To say that my aunt truly adored my husband was a huge understatement. She would brag to anyone who would listen about her big strong nephew. She was especially proud of the fact that Andre was a history professor and insisted steadfastly that he knew everything about everything.

"Do you give head?" Aunt Geraldine asked.

"What?"

"Do you suck his dick?"

"Yes Ma'am."

"How often you do that?"

"A lot."

"Um hum," Aunt Geraldine moaned, as she lit her cigar.

"Does a lot mean every time y'all have relations or what?"

"No Ma'am. Not every time."

"Do you say yes when he asks for it?"

"Yes Ma'am."

"Every time?"

I nodded my head, shamefully.

I could tell that I was about to receive some of my favorite aunt's sage advice. Aunt Geraldine was never one to shy away from any subject, no matter how risqué. She always told it to me straight and she was always right. Most people would never discuss their sex life with their parents, least of all, an old aunt who was on husband number three. Talking openly and honestly with Aunt Geraldine made me realize just how deeply painful it was for me not to have my husband totally surrender to my pleasure.

"There ain't nothing like a man with a good appetite for eating pussy," Aunt Geraldine explained. "My first husband, Frank, taught me that. I didn't know what the hell he was doing when he started. It was our wedding night, so I was dumb as a door about everything 'cause my mama didn't tell me shit about relations with a man 'cept not to do it until I was married. I was just lying there on the bed and he went down there and Jesus, I thought I was going to have a stroke. Oh, it was good!"

"Wow!" I fanned myself with a magazine. I was a bit embarrassed that I had become turned on by my aunt's vivid description.

"Jonas, my second husband," she continued while puffing away on her stogie, "wasn't that good at it. Bless his heart. He had big buck teeth and it felt like he was giving me a hysterectomy."

"What about Uncle Raymond?"

Aunt Geraldine took a long drag of the cigar before letting it dangle nonchalantly from her ruby red lips. Her round rouged cheeks bounced like rubber as she chuckled out loud.

"Well, Raymond needed a little inspiration. He was afraid of it. He hid behind that lie that Black men don't do that. That was bullshit and I knew it. Then, he said that he didn't think he would like the taste. I asked him what in the hell did he think his dick taste like? That's when I decided that I would make his favorite dessert."

"What's that?"

"Banana Pudding. I wanted to make sure that it was really good so I got the recipe from his mama. Lord knows if she had known why I really wanted it, she probably would have shot herself in the head. Anyway, I made all of his favorites for dinner one night and he ate like a broke dick dog. He said that he was too stuffed to eat another bite. I didn't fuss. I just cleaned off the kitchen table and laid down on it. I took a spoon full of his mama's banana pudding and smeared it all over my poonanny. He thought I was touched in the head but I could tell that my pussy was calling his name and he could not resist."

"What!" I exclaimed. That was the funniest story I had ever heard in my life. But listening to my aunt's detailed account of oral satisfaction made me reminisce about past lovers. None of them ever had a problem with going down on me. In fact, they seemed to enjoy it. So did I.

Just then, Uncle Raymond shuffled his way into the hot kitchen. He gave me a pat on the head and then asked Aunt Geraldine what was for supper.

"Chicken and dumplings."

"What we got sweet?" he asked, as he looked into the refrigerator.

"Banana pudding," Aunt Geraldine answered. She rolled her eyes at me for being childish and unable to control my laughter.

"Sounds good," Uncle Raymond replied as he shuffled out of the back door.

"Do you know what Andre's favorite dessert is?"

"Yes Ma'am. It's tiramisu."

"What in the hell is that?" Aunt Geraldine asked, with a confused look on her wrinkled face.

"It's an Italian dessert."

I knew that even after that simple explanation, Aunt Geraldine still would not have the slightest idea what I was talking about; although, she would never admit it.

"Oh. Well, this is what you need to do. When he comes home one night, you have his favorite meal waiting for him. Make yourself look nice with make-up and perfume and all. You spoon-feed him the entire meal like he's a baby. Make sure that you both drink plenty of liquor. You know. The brown kind. Then, you tell him about dessert. You'll know what to do next."

"I don't know about that, auntie. He may get upset."

"Trust me. The only time a man will get upset about pussy is if he ain't getting any. Make dessert for him, baby. I promise he'll ask for termite soup every night."

"Tiramisu," I corrected.

"Yea, that's what I said."

A week later, I decided I would follow my aunt's advice. She'd never steered me wrong before so I had to trust her this time. I spent all day getting ready for the event. It took over an hour and a half for me choose just the right lingerie from Victoria's Secret. The afternoon was filled with making a feast of Andre's favorite Italian foods. And for dessert, I made tiramisu.

I put one of Andre's cherished Miles Davis albums on the stereo. I dabbed a bit of perfume behind each ear and a little behind each knee. Andre was ready to jump me as soon as he walked through the door, seeing me standing there in a red lace push-up bra and silk thong.

"What's all this?" he asked, grinning from ear to ear.

"Dinner."

"Wow! Everything looks good. Especially you, baby."

"Thank you."

He sat down at the table. I sat on his lap and felt his rod lift and expand under me. I draped a linen napkin under his chin. I fed him and lovingly kissed his soft lips after every spoonful. Andre ate every heaping bite of my lasagna.

"Oh baby, that was the best meal I have ever had."

"It's not over yet. I have dessert for you."

I pulled the tiramisu from the refrigerator.

"Oh no. I can't eat another bite."

"Try a little."

I put a spoonful of the dessert in his mouth. He closed his eyes, leaned his head back and moaned deeply.

When he opened his eyes, I stuck out my tongue and placed the dessert on the tip of it. Andre slowly wrapped his slender tongue around mine and took the dessert into his mouth.

I quickly took off my bra and dabbed a little desert on my erect nipples. Andre smiled devilishly and, without question, he proceeded to take small deliberate bites.

I continued this little game with a trip down to my navel. Andre loved it. When he opened his mouth for more, I took a spoonful and smeared it on the mound of my thong. I stared expectantly and deeply into his dark eyes.

"What are you doing?"

"I'm serving you dessert, baby," I smiled. "I know it's your favorite."

"Well, um. I don't know. I mean I don't think I want to—"

"You haven't even tried it, Andre. Come on," I begged. "You know you can't resist it."

He sighed as he knelt down and licked a bit of the dessert off my thong. Then, there was another lick followed by another and another. I pulled the seat of my thong over to give Andre better access to my burning pussy. I almost came when I felt the coldness of the dessert on my swollen clit. Andre went right to work licking and sucking all of it into his mouth.

"Ooh."

"Do you like the taste of my pussy, baby?"

"Yes."

"Do you love the taste of my pussy, baby?"

"Hell yes," he moaned before he ripped off the thong.

He was a bit clumsy at first but under my careful guidance, he soon got the hang of it. He moved down to catch each drop of my sweet juice before it could fall. He slowly pushed his hot tongue inside of me.

"In and out, baby," I instructed, breathlessly.

I grabbed the back of his head and held it firmly in place as Andre worked his magic. I realized that with a little more practice, this grasshopper was well on his way to greatness.

"Yeah, right there."

He did as he was told. I felt a new sense of power as he worshipped between my legs. I was riding his tongue just as hard as I rode his dick the night before. I totally lost control and started to flood like the Ninth Ward when I caught a glimpse of our reflection in the dining room mirror.

"Goddamn!" I screamed, as I pushed his face deeper into my exploding pussy. I came in a blinding orgasmic fury.

Andre stood, licked my nectar from his lips and smiled. "Not bad. Not bad at all. I'd like more dessert, please," he said.

"No. It's my turn."

PERFECT MEASURE

He casually walked into my shop looking as fine as frog's hair. Golden brown skin, broad shoulders, a tight ass and a big smile. The sudden tingle between my legs made me realize just how long it had been since I'd had a piece of sweet dick.

"May I help you?" I asked. Even though I tried to keep my gaze above his flat stomach, I couldn't help wondering what lay beneath those stonewashed Levi's.

"Yeah. I need to have these pants hemmed," he responded, with a voice that was smooth and deep. He smiled proudly when he caught me licking my lips as I surveyed his beautiful form.

I showed him into the dressing room. The crisp clean scent of his cologne made my knees weak. The sight of his sexy silhouette through the frosted glass doors made my mouth water. I could tell from his ripped abs that he worked out. I nervously reached for my pincushion when I saw the dressing room door open, resisting the urge to rip off my clothes and throw my hot naked body on him like a wild banshee.

"They are a little too long," he pointed out.

"I can see that," I flirted back.

I knew he was talking about his pants but I was far more interested in the length of his penis.

"Okay, let me get some measurements," I said, as I pulled the tape measure from around my neck.

My heart started to pound as I knelt down in front of him. My palms sweat profusely as I ran the tape measure from the inside of his hard thigh all the way down to the top of his huge shoe. I sensed his embarrassment as his dick swelled slightly. I hoped that my own arousal would not make me lose control of my steady hand and cause me to stick him.

"Will that be all?" I asked, as I tried not to make eye contact.

I turned to write his information in my book when suddenly I felt his closeness on me.

His hardness was piercing the small of my back like a knife and his breath was hot and heavy on my neck.

"I don't know. You tell me. Is that all you need from me?" he said, low and deep.

Lord no, I thought. This man was giving me fever! I forgot about how inappropriate it would be for me to fuck a customer right here in my alterations shop; not to mention the fact that he looked young enough to be my son. But, my body needed it. I turned, opened my mouth and invited him to come in.

He kissed me hard and wild. I grabbed his sweet tongue with mine and held it until I had sucked all of the juice out of it. My flesh burned as he ripped my shirt open and ran his thick tongue slowly between my aching breasts. I unbuttoned his pants and his rock emerged like the bright sun on a brand new day. I clumsily led him into the dressing room.

"How old are you?" I asked.

"Twenty-two. Why?"

"Just making sure that what we are about to do isn't a felony because no dick is worth catching a case over." I was old enough to be his mama but I didn't give a shit. I wanted to be fucked and fucked well.

"Aren't you going to lock the door or turn on the closed sign?" he asked.

"Why? Are you scared that someone will walk in on us?"

"I'm not if you're not."

He pushed me against the mirrored walls as he continued to touch and kiss me all over. I grabbed his round ass and pulled him closer. His arms bulged as he squeezed my waist and quickly lifted me off the floor. My legs opened wide and locked effortlessly around his long and lean body.

"Hold on," he encouraged.

I flinched as he eased the head of his thickness into my hot womanhood. It had truly been too long since anyone had played there. Soon, I found my groove as he rhythmically pumped in and out of my dripping hole. Wanting him to give me more, I talked shit.

"Is that all you got?" I asked, breathlessly.

I felt his pace quicken.

"You young muthafuckas ain't shit. You call this fuckin'?"

The look in his eyes changed from relaxed to urgent. His grip on my bare ass became tighter and his once shallow thrusts became deeper and harder.

"That's what I'm talkin' about, muthafucka. Work up a sweat and fuck the shit out of me!"

"Is this what you want?" he growled.

"Shut up, you young ass muthafucka! You better not cum before I do."

I liked it hard and he was giving it to me just right. This young ass buck was wearing me out. I leaned back and balanced myself on the cutting table to allow him easy access to my sweet spot.

I started to drool when I felt my orgasm starting to rise. My juices gushed. He saw the rush of my climax in my eyes and he pounded deeper until I came with a burst of laughter and tears.

"Oh, so you think that I ain't shit? Whatcha gonna do now?" he whispered, as he exploded like an atom bomb inside of my tremoring pussy.

The cutting table held us until we had recovered.

We emerged from the dressing room and found three customers waiting. My pastor's wife stood there holding her new dress in one hand and clutching her fake ass pearls with the other.

"You can come back next Thursday and pick up your pants," I said, as he limped out of my shop.

I was worried that now young blood would start hanging around my shop like a cat after that first feeding. But, he didn't.

However, about once a month, he seemed to have a new pair of pants that needed to be hemmed.

VIBES

Dear Camille,
I hope you enjoy this gift. I spent hours picking it out just for you.
Happy Birthday!
Love,
Kyle

Camille read the handwritten note and eagerly opened the beautifully wrapped box. A smile as long as the Mississippi River emerged from her full lips when she saw what was waiting inside. It was just what she'd asked for. It sparkled like the brightest star and she instantly knew why it was called a girl's best friend.

"Kyle is a mess," she whispered, as she removed the shiny new vibrator from its velvet-lined box.

Camille examined it for a moment before gently placing it on her pillow. She admired its sleek appearance and its promise of countless hours of pleasure. She and Kyle had briefly looked at vibrators on the Internet several months earlier and joked about actually purchasing one. Camille never thought Kyle would take her request seriously but was glad he did. She knew she would have to find a way of properly thanking him for her little bunny later.

She danced to the rhythm of her own heartbeat as she lit candle after candle in her bedroom. The sweet lull of midnight love music softly playing on the radio soothed her growing anticipation. She stood in front of the long mirror that leaned against her bedroom wall and took deep cleansing breaths before letting her silk robe drop to the floor. Camille adored her body. She traced her exquisite soft brown curves with her fingertips. She closed her eyes and gently pinched each nipple, exhaling as they grew firm beneath her touch. She glanced at the gift that was waiting on her pillow. Camille's pussy walls became slick as she imagined the vibrator calling her by name.

Her clit swelled and throbbed as she reminisced about the last time she and Kyle made love.

After a long day of moving, Kyle and Camille were dog tired but wanted to christen the new house. Kyle spread blankets on the floor of the family room and lit the fireplace.

The first snow of winter created a romantic backdrop outside of the uncovered windows as their bodies melted together to celebrate their latest purchase. They took their time and savored every moment of their lovemaking. It was beautiful.

Camille climbed into bed with this memory vividly playing in her head. The coolness of the crisp sheets against her nakedness gave her goosebumps. She took her new toy in hand and slowly introduced it to her waiting wetness. She smiled as she remembered that Kyle would tease that she definitely didn't need any help in the lubrication department. Camille listened to the soft hum of her new friend and her clit delighted in making its acquaintance.

Her hot ass gyrated under its perfectly rhythmic vibrations. Her legs opened wider and she grew wetter. She took her friend into her slippery cunt deeper and soon found a spot that had never been touched by anyone. Not even by Kyle. Her body was on fire and her moans were more animalistic as her talented toy worked her inside and out. Camille realized that she was no longer in control.

Tears of joy ran down her face as her sweet juice soaked her sheets.

"Shiiiiiit!" she cried as she came like thunder in July, hard and loud.

Camille was left breathless. She became excited at the thought of doing that again, and again.

She opened her eyes and saw Kyle standing in the doorway, grinning slyly.

"Can I play, too?" he asked.

Kyle walked over, dick in hand, and planted a soft kiss on Camille's already inflamed clit. He hovered over her trembling body and eased the head his thick cock into her throbbing pussy. Because of the massive size of his rod, he'd learned to take his time when entered her.

"You are so wet, baby," Kyle whispered, as he artistically stroked the ridge of her G-spot.

Camille rotated her hips harder and faster when she realized that her second orgasm was on the horizon. She closed her eyes and allowed herself to be taken into another dimension.

The quickening of Camille's sugar walls sent Kyle over the edge and he filled her with his hot load.

"So, did you like your present?" Kyle asked, as he gently stroked her cheek.

"It's okay," Camille answered, flatly.
Kyle laughed and said, "Yeah, right."

SATISFACTION

In the beginning, I was thrilled with the whole idea of buying my first home and being Miss Independent. For the first few days after closing, I blasted the Destiny's Child tune bearing that title in my house and car. But now, that feeling had faded and reality had set in. The more I thought about it as I drove to the Home Builder's Warehouse for the fourth time in a week, the more I realized maybe I'd bit off a lot more than one do-it-yourself diva could chew. There had been problem after problem almost every day since I'd closed on the house two months ago. It was a blown fuse that had brought me to the store the day before. The day before that, the kitchen faucet needed a washer. And, a week before that, I had to purchase a brand new front door to replace the one that was rotting from years of neglect. I was beginning to think that this nightmare fixer-upper and its steady stream of needed repairs were going to totally bleed my savings account dry before I could get to the improvements that I actually wanted to make.

"What brings you in today, Ms. Baldwin?" the cashier asked as I walked through the automatic doors. It was a damn shame that I had been in the store so many times that most of the staff knew me by name.

"I need to pick up a dryer coil and some numbers for my mailbox," I answered as I grabbed a red hand basket.

"Let us know if you need help with anything."

Yeah, yeah, I thought as I sighed deeply and headed down the aisles to find what I needed. I was truly growing weary of this home ownership shit. It was much easier when I lived in an apartment and could just pick up the phone and call the maintenance guy whenever there was a problem with anything. Now everything from making the monthly mortgage payment to cutting the grass was all on me. Unfortunately, there was no significant man in my life who I could call to take care of these things for me. My father died two years ago and I had no brothers or cousins who could be bothered, let alone, trusted to do anything in my home. My last romantic relationship lasted four years and ended six months before Clinton left the White

House. I came home early from work one day to surprise my live-in lover with a little afternoon delight. I walked into our bedroom and caught some trifling skank bitch, sporting fake titties and a cheap weave with her head between my boyfriend's legs. After kicking both of their asses out and spending a night in jail, I decided to give up on men.

Period.

This wasn't the first time in my life that I'd been a woman scorned. Men were just more trouble than they were worth in my book. I no longer had the patience or the inclination to deal with all of the drama. When I first told my best friend, Angel, about my decision to be manless, she was mortified.

"You ain't fixin' to turn into a lesbian after only one night in the joint, are you? I love you like a sister, but I can't deal with that."

"No, Angel. I mean that I'm not going to date anyone," I explained, "I'm going to concentrate on me, myself, and I for a minute."

"Humph, no man? No dick? You are going to be quite the bitch to be around," Angel concluded. "Thanks for the warning."

"I will be just fine as long as my Costco membership remains up-to-date and I can buy all the batteries that I need to keep my little bunny rabbit humming along."

Truth was being celibate was going to be a lot harder than I let on and too much responsibility for one vibrator to handle. I made a mental note to order a new one.

After I found the dryer coil and was on my way to the next aisle, I decided to stop and take a peek at the beautiful flooring that was on sale. I knew that at the rate I was going, it would be months maybe even years before I could afford an extravagant purchase like new floors for the house even though it was something that the entire house really needed. I ran my fingers over the textured carpets that seemed to be available in every color of the rainbow. I picked up a square of the ceramic tile and was amazed with all the different design options it presented. Ceramic tile was actually a project I felt that I could realistically tackle by myself, I thought as I moved over to the hardwood flooring display.

"May I help you?"

I turned to see who was talking to me and was greeted by a man with a smile that was as wide as the Atlantic and as bright as Orion at midnight.

"Um, not really. I'm just looking and fantasizing."

"Well, there's nothing wrong with a little fantasy, now is there?"

"No, I suppose not. But I can't afford hardwood floors right now," I answered as I began to walk toward the mailbox aisle.

"Wait a minute. Don't give up so easily. How do you know you can't afford it," the man asked, grabbing my elbow as he gently pulled me back.

"Because I know how much money there is in my bank account."

I decided to get a better look at this man who was getting all up in my business. Of all the times that I've been in this store, I couldn't remember ever seeing him. Damn, I thought. This was one fine ass brother! The small diamond stud in his ear sparkled in perfect harmony with his bald head and rich mahogany skin.

"Are you aware of our many financing options? If you really want hardwood floors, there is more than one way to pay for them," he explained, "We can design something that will be pleasing to the eye as well as to your pocketbook."

As I listened to him, my eyes quickly surveyed his body.

"Mr…"

"Call me Troy."

"Okay, Troy. I am a single woman who is barely making the mortgage payments on the house to begin with, so I definitely ain't trying to open no new credit accounts right now. But thanks anyway."

"Single huh? Well, like I said, there is more than one way to get what you want. Tell you what. Why don't you let me come by and measure your house? After we get an accurate measurement, you'll know exactly what dollar amount we're dealing with," Troy offered.

"I don't know about that. It really doesn't matter because I have no money."

"The estimate is free and if you find that you really can't afford it, you're only out of a few minutes of your time," he insisted.

"Okay, what the hell. You did say the estimate was free, right?"

"Yes ma'am," Troy said, smiling.

I knew that there was no way in hell that I would be able to afford any new floors, but Troy just wouldn't let it go. I gave him my address and phone number just to get him off my back. Quite frankly, he was so persistent that he could have probably talked me out of my panties right there on the showroom floor.

I had forgotten all about Troy and the hardwood floor until two days later. Just as I was pulling my car into the garage after a long day at work, I heard the phone ringing. I rushed inside to answer it and it was Troy. The sound of his velvety voice made my heart race and my girl parts tingle.

"Ms. Baldwin? This is Troy from the flooring department at Home Builder's Warehouse."

"Yes, Troy. How are you?"

"I'm great. Thank you. I'm calling to set up a time for me to come out to your home and take those measurements we discussed. When would be a good time for a busy woman like you?" he asked, charming me again.

I really wanted to tell him to forget it because I was short on time and even shorter on cash.

"Well, how about Saturday morning?" I offered as I rolled my eyes.

"Saturday morning is perfect. Say, about ten-thirty?"

"Yep, that'll work."

After the disastrous day I'd had at work, I was in no mood to negotiate. I hung up the phone with Troy and then called to order take-out from the Greek restaurant around the corner. The sooner I ate, the sooner I could take a hot shower and go straight to bed.

After I read a chapter of a novel that I'd pick up from the library last week, I said a quick prayer and turned off the lights. As I lay there, I found myself thinking about Troy. I wondered if he was in a relationship with anyone. As fine as he was, there had to be a woman out there somewhere with his name tattooed all over her sweet spot.

I also wondered what kind of lover he was. Was he a slow grinding soul stirrer or a fast humping body snatcher? I thought about how I'd noticed the size of his hands as he filled out the information card the other day. They were as big as bricks and I began to imagine them wrapped around my thick waist. I could tell that Troy worked out. He was big enough to take a hearty thrust from a big girl and not go flying across the room. I closed my eyes and squeezed my rock hard nipple at the memory of the sound of his sexy deep voice. My body shuddered with waves of ecstasy, and I could almost smell his sweet cologne on the pillow next to me.

The urge to touch and fondle my already throbbing clit was strong and unyielding. I couldn't resist dipping my fingers deep into my honey pot and writing Troy's name on the spot where I wished he could be. Writhing wildly on my baby blue Egyptian cotton sheets, my strokes became harder and more urgent until I came and practically set my bed on fire. I lay there, satisfied for now, as the quickening of my womanhood lulled me into a peaceful sleep.

Saturday morning arrived accompanied by showers and thunderstorms. I loved rainy days because they forced me to stay home and get some chores done instead of running errands all over town.

As I snuggled on the paisley chaise with my favorite throw and my cat, Blue, on my lap, my thoughts turned to Troy again. I couldn't believe how fine this man was and how he had occupied every nook and cranny of my mind ever since he'd called to set up the appointment a few days ago. Since I made my decision to be celibate, I have never felt this strongly about another man, especially one that I barely knew. I realized that the reason for his visit today was supposed to be strictly business, but there were a few personal questions that I needed to have answered.

My phone rang and I knew it had to be Troy calling to cancel. Surely, he wasn't going to attempt to come out in this storm. I instantly felt disappointed.

"Ms. Baldwin, this is Troy."

"Hello Troy." I could tell from the sound of screeching windshield wipers that he was calling from his cell phone.

"Yes, I am on my way out to your home right now. It's going to take a little longer than I expected because of the rain."

"Troy, you don't have to come out in this weather just to give me an estimate. We can always reschedule," I lied. I knew how badly I wanted to have this man in my house today.

"Nonsense. I'll be there in about twenty minutes."

This man is serious about his work, I thought as I hung up the phone and put on a fresh pot of coffee. I figured that Troy would need something warm to drink after schlepping around in this cold and rainy weather. Actually, I thought of a lot of warm things Troy could have, if he so desired.

A few minutes later, I noticed a black Jeep Grand Cherokee slowly passing by my house before stopping and then backing into my driveway. I laughed out loud when I noticed his personalized license plate that read "2Screw".

I didn't wait for Troy to ring the doorbell. I opened the door and watched him gather some supplies from the back of his SUV before coming inside.

"Good rainy morning, Ms. Baldwin," he greeted as he shook the water from his now closed umbrella.

"Good morning to you, too," I responded, directing him through the door.

He stopped and removed his black steel toed boots and placed them in the vinyl shoe tray in the front hallway before moving on to the living room. I gave him an A+ for being considerate of my home without being asked.

"Oh my, Ms. Baldwin. This is a truly beautiful house. May I ask how long you've owned it?"

Blue playfully flirted between his legs, begging to be picked up. I chuckled to myself because like Blue, I, too, wanted to play between Troy's legs.

"Please call me, Alicia. I bought it two months ago."

"It has great architecture. Most older homes do. Do you mind if I look around a bit before I get started with your estimate?"

"Not at all. Would you like a cup of coffee? I just made a fresh pot," I asked. I felt a little embarrassed when I realized that I had been so obsessed with my thoughts of Troy that I had forgotten to get dressed. I was still wearing my pink and purple Hello Kitty flannel pajamas and matching slippers. Well, at least I'd showered the night before or I would have really been embarrassed.

"A cup of coffee would be great. I need something to warm me up," he said as he ran his big beautiful black hands across my countertops.

"It's only laminate. I'd love to replace them with black granite one day. But that's something else on the list that I can't afford right now," I explained.

"If you'd like, I could go ahead and take measurements for the countertops while I'm here. I took the liberty of bringing a few flooring samples with me. I could also pull some granite samples. That way, you can choose the finish you want and you'll know exactly what kind of money you're looking at."

"Okay. Might as well. But I have a feeling that all of this is just a waste of your time because I know that I can't afford any of it. How do you take your coffee?"

"You'll be surprised at the many low payment options we offer to fit any budget. There is more than one way to get what you want. As for my coffee, my only requirement is that it is hot, sweet and black," he said, smiling.

My heart was racing and I wasn't sure if it was because of the caffeine from the strong coffee or Troy's last answer. After I handed Troy his cup, I followed him around from room to room, explaining their purpose and my future plans for each of them. Troy was a wealth of information on how to transform a space on a shoestring budget. I was excited about the fact that all of his wonderful ideas were things that I could actually do myself.

During our tour, I made a few observations of my own. Troy was not wearing a wedding ring, but I realized that didn't necessarily mean that he wasn't married. His tight faded jeans were neatly pressed and hugged his booty perfectly. The black long-sleeved Under Armor shirt revealed a landscape of hardworking biceps. I could barely contain the strong urge to touch him. From my estimation, Troy was about six-foot-seven, and he walked with the same confident black man swagger as Samuel L. Jackson.

"This is the master bedroom," I said. "Forgive the mess. It is Saturday morning, after all and quite honestly, I'd still be in bed if you weren't here."

"There was no need to get out of bed on my account," Troy said as he turned to me and smiled slyly.

No he didn't say that, I thought. We could both strip down right now and jump in and sweat the day away between the sheets.

"I'm sure your wife hated to see you leave the house on a cold wet morning like today. Days like this are tailor made for snuggling," I began to investigate.

"That would be a problem if I actually had a wife."

Hmm, no wife, I noted.

"Alicia, do you plan to install hardwood flooring throughout the entire house or just in your public living spaces?"

"I want hardwood floors in all of the rooms except in the bathrooms, of course."

"What are your plans for those rooms?"

"Ceramic or porcelain tile."

"Great choices. Either would work just fine."

Troy took out a small memo pad and began jotting something down. I licked my lips at the sight of those hands. I closed my eyes and prayed that there was some truth in the myth about men with big hands. When I opened my eyes, I noticed a bulge in Troy's pants that made my face hot.

"Okay. Let's get started. I'll measure your countertops first, then we'll move to the floors. How's that?"

The sight of the enormous package in his pants left me speechless. I nodded yes. At that moment, he pulled the measuring tape from his front pocket and I realized that I had become all excited for nothing.

I remained in my bedroom checking emails and placed an order for a new vibrator while Troy meandered through the house clicking and clacking his measuring tape. He returned to the bedroom for the final floor measurement. I sighed with disappointing anticipation when he finally put away his tape and pulled out his calculator.

"Don't start deep breathing yet," he joked, "let's see what we have here first. Do you mind if I sit on your bed while I figure this all out?"

"No. Go ahead." This was actually the closest a man had been to my bed in years.

Hmm, Sean John cologne, I noted.

I watched as Troy added, multiplied and divided number after number and I knew it was all going to equal "no way" for me.

"Here's what we've got, Alicia. For the granite countertops in the kitchen, you're looking at about seventeen-fifty. The hardwood flooring is going to run you another five grand plus tax and labor."

I burst into an uncontrollable laughter. There was no way in hell that I had six thousand dollars to put into this house right now.

"I'm so sorry, Troy, but it seems as if you've wasted a great deal of your time. Like I told you at the store, I can't afford it," I explained, after regaining my composure.

"There you go, again. Speculating. Just hold on a minute. Maybe I could help you out," he begged.

"The only way I'll be able to afford all of this is if I steal it. Are you talking about giving me the five finger discount?"

"Alicia, even though I work for Home Builder's Warehouse, I also do a little work on the side."

"Bootleg?" I laughed again.

"No, not bootleg. I'm a licensed contractor and I do great work. I could lay these floors for you myself and save you some money. The same is true for the countertops. I could buy all of the materials for you and use my employee discount, saving you additional money."

"Why would you do that? You don't know me?"

"Maybe because I'm a nice guy who understands how difficult it is to make ends meet these days. Or, maybe I'd just love to help out a beautiful woman who needs to have floors laid."

His tone had changed. Now his voice was sexier than ever and filled with infinite possibilities. I decided that since Troy had been bold enough to reveal his agenda, I should match it with a revelation of my own.

"Floors aren't the only things around here that need to be laid and my countertops aren't the only things I would like in granite," I said, blowing ever so slightly over my mug without ever breaking eye contact with him.

"Is that right?" Troy smiled and put his notebook down on the bed and moved in closer to me. The sweet redolence of his cologne dizzied me. "Well, like I said earlier, there is more than one way to get what you want."

"Any suggestions?" I closed my laptop and rested it on my nightstand in anticipation of Troy's kiss. The initial touch of his lips on mine shot through me like lightning and ignited a fire inside that had been extinguished for far too long. Our tongues found each other and became instant friends.

"Before we go any further, I have a confession to make," Troy began.

Oh shit, here we go, I thought. I knew there had to be something.

"The other day was not the first time that I noticed you, Alicia. I've been admiring you since the first time you walked into the store."

"What? But I don't remember seeing you until..."

"That's because I was busy setting up the flooring displays with a few other guys. I saw you and I liked what I saw."

"Oh really?" My desire to have this man grew as I listened to him.

"Yes, really. The first day you came in, you were wearing a Race for the Cure T-shirt and black jeans. Your twists were pulled back into a ponytail."

I couldn't believe it. He was right.

"All I could think about was how I wished I was lucky enough to have that round ass all to myself every night," Troy continued.

"Looks like today may be your lucky day."

My mind went blank and my breaths became shallow when I felt Troy's hand on the top button of my shirt. His tongue playfully trailed its way down from my earlobe to my tight nipple. A surge of moisture from my pulsating pussy confirmed my belief that I wanted and needed to be fucked and fucked well.

I grabbed his shirt and pulled it over his head and quickly proceeded to unbuckle his 501's and realized that he had exceeded my expectations. Troy was hung like the harvest moon. Everything about this man's body was so smooth and hard that I had to touch and kiss each and every part just to make sure that it was real. He moaned softly as I gently pinched the head of his swollen dick.

"Do you taste as beautiful as you look?" Troy asked as he nibbled at my neck.

"I don't know. You tell me," I answered; I removed my pajama bottoms and opened my legs wide.

Troy kissed and lightly sucked the inside of my thick brown thighs. My entire body shook uncontrollably with the touch of his hot tongue to my bud.

"Sss...aah, Troy," I whispered while stroking his scalp as he worshiped between my legs, "this shit is so fucking good."

I wrapped my shapely legs around his torso and bucked harder and faster when I felt the dawning of what promised to be the most incredible orgasm. Troy continued to devour my pussy as I came and almost snapped his neck.

Troy stood, smiled and licked the nectar that was dripping from his lips.

"Your sweet juice is intoxicating," he said as he planted a bit of it on my lips with his kiss.

I reached into the top drawer of my nightstand and pulled out a condom and passed it to Troy. I was glad that even though I wasn't getting any dick, I still kept an emergency stash of rubbers close by just in case. Working for Planned Parenthood definitely had its privileges.

"Put this on and let's see what else you can get into."

"Why don't you put it on for me?"

"Anything to oblige a guest."

Troy leaned his head back and hissed like a snake as I licked the length of his heavy meat before rolling the ribbed rubber onto it. Before I knew it, Troy had effortlessly mounted me and slid his steel rod inside of my slick reservoir.

"Goddamn," I screamed with delight at the first smooth stroke.

The look of sheer pleasure on his face coupled with his deep soulful moans told me that he had found heaven inside me with each thrust. Each passionate kiss on my neck and sensuous suck of my breast sent me flying over the rainbow.

I closed my eyes and opened my legs as wide as the ocean so that I wouldn't miss an inch of his great and powerful dick. He descended deeper and deeper into my cave and began to feed the hungry beast that had been living inside me for so long. Every time his thick head grazed my G-spot, I felt as if I would flood and drown us both.

"Oh shit. Stay right there," I said, hoarsely, enjoying the tune Troy's thick balls played as they beat against my hot ass like a drum.

"You like that?"

"Yeah."

"Your pussy is so damn good and soaking wet, baby. You like the way I'm fucking you?"

"Oh yeah," I answered, breathlessly.

I couldn't remember having a dick this hard moving inside of me. This was the best fuck I had ever had in my life. Troy rode me with the sensuous precision of a masterfully trained stallion hitting its stride. Our burning bodies melted into each other like milk chocolate on Alabama concrete as the rain poured outside my window. The thunderstorm that raged outside provided the perfect soundtrack for the fire that was raging inside my bedroom.

"Oh shit, Oh shit..."

"Come on, tell me what you want."

"Fuck the shit out of me, Troy!"

"You love this big dick, don't you?"

"Hell yes!"

My muted moans turned to banshee screams as Troy tore my pussy up. Our rhythmic gyrations were in perfect harmony. I felt the beginning of that familiar eruption at my core. I dug my fingernails into Troy's ass and tried to push him deeper as he worked his groove.

"Ahh...shit," Troy growled, as his pace quickened.

"Troy," I yelled.

"Shit..."

I exploded in what felt like a never-ending orgasm that sent me on a high like I had ever experienced. My pulsating sugar walls saturated Troy's dick with my love syrup.

"I can't hold this shit, Alicia," Troy whispered in my ear.

"Cum hard for me, Troy."

He pumped me harder and faster like a well-oiled machine. Troy roared like a lion as he released his thick full load of pleasure.

Troy kissed me deeply as we both lay totally exhausted yet immensely satisfied from loving and fell asleep in each other's arms.

Awakened by the sound of the shower, I turned and sat up in bed. Where in the hell was Troy going, I wondered. Was he going home after he'd played in my playground all morning long?

"Are you leaving, Troy?" I asked, feeling myself becoming pissed.

"Yes. I've got to get going. I have quite a bit of work to do today," he said as he pulled on his jeans.

I jumped out of bed like someone had lit a firecracker in my ass.

"Work? I don't recall you mentioning any work while you were fucking my brains out. Now that you've got what you wanted, you've got work to do? I knew it. I knew. You're just like every other goddamn man. Selfish ass motherfucker! You know what? It's my own damn fault for giving up my pussy to some goddamn handyman that I don't even know. Get the fuck out of my goddamn house, Troy!"

I couldn't believe that I was standing in my bathroom, butt-naked, screaming and cussing. It was also unbelievable that I had allowed my horniness to cause me to do something so stupid. I felt weak and embarrassed, and I wanted to cry, but I was not going to give Troy the satisfaction.

"Um, Alicia? Can I explain something to you?" Troy interrupted, while looking perplexed.

"What is it, Troy?" I yelled. "What the fuck is it?"

"I need to go to Home Builder's Warehouse to pick up the supplies I need to get started on your floors. While you were asleep, I called ahead and ordered the hardwood because I want to start installing them today."

"Oh," I said, feeling like a complete idiot for going off on Troy like a crazy woman.

"Yeah, I'm waiting. You can apologize any time you're ready," Troy said, jokingly as he grabbed me around the waist and pulled me closer to him.

"I'm so sorry, Troy. It's just..."

"No explanation necessary, baby. I understand."

"But how are you going to get supplies when I don't have any money to give you?"

Troy kissed me on my forehead very sweetly and lifted my chin with his hand.

"You've given me all I need. If we're going to be spending time together, I might as well start earning my keep and create a home that is as beautiful as the woman who owns it."

"Oh, you assume that I'm going to let you spend time here?" I asked sarcastically.

"Oh, I know you will."

"And how do you know that?"

"Because after the whooping you've just put on me, I ain't going to be that easy to get rid of, love," Troy said as he cupped my bare ass in the palm of his hand.

As I showered and waited for Troy to return, I couldn't stop smiling. This man was habit-forming and I believed that I was hooked.

The next few months with Troy were like heaven on earth. Just as he'd promised, Troy installed hardwood floors and granite countertops along with finishing up a few more needed repairs around the house. In the process, we fell deeply in love. I admit, I was skeptical in the beginning about opening up my heart to another man, but I realized that I couldn't live my life punishing every man that I met for the failures of a few worthless sonsof-bitches. Troy was different. His love was real, and I could feel it with each kiss and I could see it in each glance. I knew that I could trust him with my heart.

I knew we were becoming an old married couple without being married when we painted my bedroom on my birthday.

"Alicia, I have something very special to give you," he said, nervously.

He was holding a gray plastic Home Builder's Warehouse bag. I had no idea what was inside. Troy's hand was trembling and tiny beads of sweat formed on his forehead.

"Are you okay?" I asked as I took the bag.

"Yeah, I'm cool. Just open the bag."

When I opened the bag, there was a chocolate brown suede tool belt inside. My face instantly became hot. I knew good and hell well that Troy was not giving me this shit for my birthday. The expression on my paint-smeared face must have said as much because Troy quickly instructed me to pull out the tool belt.

"What the hell is this, Troy?"

"Turn it around."

I reluctantly did as I was told and saw my name embroidered on the hammer pocket. Okay, now I was really pissed.

"It matches mine. See?" Troy said, proudly grinning as he pointed to the tool belt he was wearing.

What? Was he for real? Just as I opened my mouth to cuss him out, something in one of the pockets of the belt caught my attention. At first, I thought it was a pretty little decorative screw. When I reached inside, I realized that it wasn't a screw at all but the most gorgeous antique diamond ring that I had ever seen in my life. Now, my hands were trembling uncontrollably. Troy took the ring from my hand and got down on one knee. He didn't even notice that he was kneeling in a roller pan of lavender paint.

"Alicia, when I first saw you, I knew that you were special. The first time we made love, I felt your beautiful spirit. Now, I feel that my soul has truly found a resting place. Will you be my wife?"

I was speechless. I never in a million years expected a proposal.

"Yes, Troy. I would love to be your wife," I answered through the curtain of tears that ran down my face.

Troy kissed my quivering lips. He slid the diamond ring onto my stained finger and wrapped the tool belt around my waist.

At that moment, I realized that all was right with the world. Troy was the man that fate had designed just for me.

THE RIDE

It is big, black, and easily able to handle the ride of a thick madame like me, and when I turn it on, I know it will return the favor, I thought as I looked out of my bedroom window and took a sip of my coffee. I had been eagerly anticipating the arrival of my spanking brand new Cadillac Escalade for weeks, and now that the big event was just moments away, I could barely contain my excitement.

For the first time in my life, I was able to buy a car and have it fully customized to fit my personal diva style. The best part of it all was that I paid cash for it without hesitation. My career as an author was finally beginning to pay off royally, enabling me to do a lot of things that, at one time, seemed virtually impossible. Being a smart, beautiful, and successful Black woman made me feel as if the world was now at my manicured fingertips.

Once upon a time, I thought about the possibility of giving up the single life and settling down into marital bliss. It was not as if I'd had a shortage of prospects and proposals. My problem was that at thirty-four, I'd become so used to doing me without having to ask permission or seek approval, I think that it would be difficult for me to do things differently. My best friend had been married for five years and before she could even commit to having lunch with me on a Tuesday afternoon, she had to check to make sure that it was okay with her husband. To me, that just seems utterly ridiculous. On the flip side of that, she couldn't understand the fact that I was enjoying my life without having a man shackled to my ankle.

"Girl, I think that deep down inside, you want to be married but there is something you are afraid of," she'd always say.

I'm not afraid of anything. From what I'd seen out there, commitment ain't all people made it out to be. I'd seen too many sisters' lives destroyed by trying to hold on to someone who no longer wanted to be held. I loved my life just the way it was. Besides, the fuck 'em and leave 'em game wouldn't be half as much fun if I were somebody's ball and chain.

Waiting for the car to arrive was driving me insane, so I decided to go into the kitchen and cook myself a little breakfast, hoping to take my mind off of the fact that the salesman was late with the delivery of my precious new baby. And what a cute salesman he was. His eyes were dark and mysterious and his chocolate brown skin was flawless and smooth. The Rock of Gibraltar seriously paled in comparison to the hardness of this man's ass. Even though the nature of our relationship was strictly business, the air between us was definitely heavy with flirtation. I welcomed the opportunity to get to know him a whole lot better, and I sensed he felt the same. The memories of our first meeting flooded my mind and instantly brought a smile to my face.

"So, Ms. James, why do you want an Escalade? It is a big vehicle," he said during my test-drive. "Are you sure that you can handle an SUV of this size?"

"Well, I want a big vehicle 'cause I'm a big girl and I need something that will more than adequately reflect the style of its beautifully voluptuous owner," I answered as I leaned closer, allowing him to get a better view of the depth of my cleavage. He was instantly hypnotized by the slight reveal of my black lace push-up bra that confidently held the eighth and ninth wonders of the world beneath my white sheer silk blouse. "And as far as the size goes, well, I so believe that bigger is definitely better."

"How do you like the way the SUV handles the road? Cadillac has done a great job of manufacturing a sports utility vehicle that still maintains the luxury that is synonymous with the brand," he continued, trying hard to remain the consummate professional.

"I absolutely love it."

"One of the favorite and most popular features of the car is the heated seats. They are great for warming you up on those cold winter mornings. And, of course, they are standard."

"Heated seats, huh? I don't think I'll be needing those," I said, laughing and rubbing my ample ass. "My seat has no problem staying hot enough on its own."

"Well, for 2009, Cadillac has introduced cooled seats. Also standard," he continued after clearing his throat. It appeared as if I was making him uncomfortable.

"Now that feature alone is reason enough to purchase this car," I joked. "Lord knows that there are days that I need to cool off my seat, even when I'm not driving.

"You have selected the Hybrid model, Ms. James. I'm sure that I don't have to tell you that even though you will pay a little more for a hybrid vehicle upfront, the savings over the long run will be well worth it," he continued to explain.

Is this man clueless? Did he hear what I just said? He is not responding to my overtures at all. This is new. He must be married. I don't see a wedding ring or any evidence of band tan that is usually noticeable when married men remove their rings.

The citrusy scent of his cologne was wickedly intoxicating. I closed my eyes and inhaled the sensuously sexiness of the stud sitting next to me. His voice trailed into the distance and my imagination went into sexual overdrive as I began to visualize all of the ways in which I could make this man scream my name.

Look at his lips. I wonder if he eats pussy. I bet he does. Lips like those are perfect for devouring pussy like a vulture. I could see us dancing the sixty-nine. He would bury his face deep into my muff, and I would grind on his tongue like my life depended on it. I bet his dick would feel right at home in the warmth of my mouth. I would suck it until it was bone dry, swallowing all of its succulent juices.

"Ms. James...helloo...Ms. James. Are you okay?" I heard the salesman call, jolting me from my naughty thoughts.

"Huh...what...yes, yes, of course, I'm okay. I'm so sorry."

"Are you sure? You seemed so far away. What were you thinking about?"

Oh how I wish I could tell you.

"I was just fantasizing about having you...I mean...having this car all to myself," I lied. I quickly realized that I had become way too caught up in my daydream when I looked down and saw my right hand pumping the gearshift like it was his dick. Even though he didn't let on, I knew that he noticed it, too.

When we arrived back at the dealership, we went into his office to fine-tune the delicate details of the transaction. I quickly surveyed his desk and credenza for pictures of a loving wife, devoted girlfriend, or any significant other probabilities. The only picture adorning the small room was one of him sporting a broad grin while sitting on a sandy beach with his arm around a beautiful Golden Retriever.

"What a beautiful dog," I admired.

"Thanks. That's Memphis."

"Memphis?"

"Yeah, that's where I grew up."

That is corny as hell.

"You named your dog after your hometown? That's cute. He looks like a great family dog. Your kids must love him," I pried. I needed to make sure that this candidate was properly vetted before I could move on with my plans.

"I'm sure he would be a great family dog if I had a family," he quickly answered.

No kids.

As I walked around the office, checking out the framed degree from Vanderbilt University along with several "Salesman of the Month" awards that hung proudly on the walls, I felt the heat of his stare on each and every curve of my body.

"So, Mr. Grant, you're not married?" I asked as I turned and caught him seductively licking his lips.

"It's Damon and the answer to your question is no. I am not married."

"Girlfriend?"

"No."

"Boyfriend?"

"Absolutely not," he replied, laughing this time. Damon's rich full-bodied voice sent an immediate surge of electricity down my spine.

"My, don't you ask a lot of questions, Ms. James."

"Damon, I'm about to write you a check for a great deal of money. I need to know all there is to know about the potential recipient."

"Oh, I see," he replied, leaning back in his black leather chair. "Well, do you mind if I ask you a few questions?"

"Not at all. I'm an open book," I answered. I sat down in the black leather chair across from his desk and crossed my shapely caramel legs, allowing for a slight rise in my skirt. The peekaboo view of my black thong made him stutter.

"Umm... well... are you married, engaged, or dating?" he asked, trying extremely hard but unsuccessfully not to stare at my thick calves.

"No, no, and no."

Damon cleared his throat and flashed a full smile that appeared to be ten miles wide, indicating that he was clearly pleased with my responses.

"Any prospects?"

Licking my glossed lips, I answered, "Well, I've got my eye on a sexy car salesman."

"Is that right?"

His voice was different now. It was even deeper and sexier. In it, I heard the definite possibility of falling asleep in Damon's arms at night and waking him with plenty of good loving and good food in the morning.

"That is exactly right," I answered, taking off my panties and tossing them onto the purchase order form on the desk in front of him. Damon's eyes widened and his forehead began to secrete tiny beads of sweat.

"Ms. James..." he said as he lifted the thong with his pen.

"Yes?"

"This is highly inappropriate. We have to maintain a professional relationship. You have to put your panties back on."

"You know that you can barely resist the urge to inhale the scent of my sex. Go ahead. Do it. No one is watching."

"I can't, Ms. James. Please, put your underwear back on before my manager walks in," he begged and then threw them back into my lap. I couldn't believe that he was turning down what I know to be the sweetest pussy on the planet.

"No. I prefer not to," I said as I opened my shapely legs even wider, modeling the thin hairy strip that led the way to my treasure cove. "I know that you want to look."

"You know what? Let's just go ahead and finish up here," he stuttered.

"Fine with me."

He can't be gay. If he is, it is a damn waste of good dick.

"What do you do for a living, Ms. James?" he asked.

"I'm an author."

"An author? Really? That's interesting. What genre?"

I smiled and allowed my hazel brown eyes to lock with his.

"Erotica."

"Oh really?"

"Really."

"Where do you get the inspiration for your stories?"

I knew you couldn't resist. You do want to fuck me. I don't know why you are playing games. But if a game is what you want...

"Here and there," I answered. I immediately knew what his next question would be. It's what people, especially men, always ask me when I tell them the type of stories I write.

"Are any of your stories written about personal experiences?"

Bingo! I knew it. Same question.

"A few."

I could tell from the curious look on Damon's beautiful face that my response intrigued him. For the rest of the afternoon, I asked and answered a lot of questions. Some of them actually concerned the major purchase I was about to make.

After I laid out the custom features I wanted, like the red monogrammed driver's side headrest and the twelve disk CD magazine, Damon said that it would take a few weeks to get it all done. He then volunteered to personally deliver the automobile to my home.

"Maybe you'll let me take you for a ride when you deliver the car," I seductively offered, hoping that he would understand exactly what I meant.

"I'm looking forward to it," he answered, rising from his seat for the first time since we'd entered his office. One look at the mouthwatering bulge that was barely contained by his zipper and I knew why he had remained seated.

Mmm...I bet you are hung like a Brahma bull.

I took my panties and tucked them into the pocket of his blue shirt.

"One whiff of my essence and I promise, you won't be able to think about anything else," I whispered as I put on my Chanel sunglasses and sashayed out of the dealership.

I truly expected him to call me after that but he didn't. Maybe I read him wrong. Maybe he was gay. Or maybe he just didn't find me alluring.

Naw, that's not it. That can't be it. I mean, look at me.

I knew that I was, without a doubt, the finest woman he had ever laid his eyes on. Perhaps Damon was the kind of man who liked to make the first move, the one who was the chaser. I may have been too aggressive with him but I couldn't help it. When I wanted a man, I had no problem letting him know how much. Usually, that worked in my favor. But not with Damon.

Oh well. I gambled and I lost this time. I wonder if a second chance to woo Damon is even possible now. Can I play the role of a coy lady to get what I want? It will be tough but I'm always up for a challenge.

I was instantly snapped out of my memories of that day by the sound of someone continuously blowing a car horn. I ran to the living room window and saw Damon smiling, standing in my driveway with one hand on the steering wheel and the other waving in the air.

Oh shit! It's here!

I opened the door and ran outside, forgetting to properly tighten the belt on my short red silk robe. I wasn't sure if it was the excitement of finally getting my car or the crispness of the late October morning air that caused my nipples to expand.

"Good morning, Ms. James."

"Good morning," I said, not making eye contact with him. I couldn't take my focus off of the exquisite vehicle that was parked in front of my house. Besides, I wasn't interested in playing any more games with Damon. He'd already proven himself to be too damn shy for me.

It seems as if I've been waiting for you my whole life.

"Well, Ms. James, she's all yours," he said as he walked around the vehicle, shaking the keys in my direction.

"Please, call me Jada. Wow, it is hard to believe that the car is finally here," I said, actively fondling the Cadillac emblem on the front grill that sparkled in the morning sun. I realized that I had been so enamored of the car that I hadn't paid any attention to the fine specimen who delivered it. Damon looked stunningly masculine in his charcoal grey dress pants and lavender button down shirt.

I don't think that I've ever seen a brother wearing this color combination before. I like it. Are those Prada sunglasses he's wearing? Is he gay or just metro-sexual?

He appeared a little bit thicker than I remembered. Not fat. Just packed full of hard muscle, and that was just fine with me. I was what some would call a big woman, and I loved big men who could hold their own when I started bucking. I'd tried the skinny man thing before and it never worked. I always seemed to toss their little asses around like ragdolls and sent them flying across the room. I didn't think that would be a problem with this one. His coffee colored skin looked so sweet and luxurious that it was hard to resist the urge to touch it.

Hmm...there's that delightful scent again. My panties would be completely soaked if I were actually wearing any.

"Thank you so much for getting her home to me safely. I really appreciate it. Would you like to come inside for a cup of coffee, or do you have to get back to the dealership?"

"Actually, today is my day off."

"What? You delivered my car on your day off? Damon, you didn't have to do that. I'm glad you did, but you didn't have to," I said, taking his strong hand into mine.

Remember, slow it down. You have to let him take the lead.

"I promised to deliver the car to you as soon as it came in, and I couldn't break a promise to a beautiful woman and still sleep peacefully at night," he said, smiling.

"Well, in that case, you will not only come inside for coffee but I think you deserve an omelet and some French toast," I said as I led him inside.

"What about the car? Have you forgotten that you promised to take me for a ride?"

"No. I haven't forgotten. I'll take you for a ride after we eat."

I'm not going to let you get away this time.

We talked non-stop as I prepared Damon's morning feast. The conversation was exciting as we effortlessly moved from one topic to the next. I loved the way he made me laugh.

"Jada, I'd really like to read your work sometime," Damon admitted.

"Are you sure? I mean, I'd love for you to read it but remember, it is erotica. Not everyone can handle the heat," I warned.

"Oh, heat is my specialty."

Is he flirting back with me? Well, it is about damn time. For a minute, I thought I was losing my touch.

I decided to start him out with one of my milder creations. I handed him a copy of Playgirl magazine where one of my short stories was featured. The illustration alone caused Damon to raise an eyebrow. He read the piece without making a sound.

"Wow, your writing is bold," he said as he smiled and closed the magazine.

"Bold is what people should expect when they read erotica. It is not Mother Goose, for Christ's sake."

"You are right about that. I really like the story, Jada. I must admit that I have not read a lot of erotica. Men tend to be more visual, you know. If we can't actually see the nude woman, it sometimes gets lost on us. But your descriptions are very vivid and I like that. Congratulations on your success."

"Thank you, Damon. Well, here you go. One ham and cheese omelet with banana stuffed French toast and warm maple syrup," I announced as I placed the plate on the table in front of him and laid a blue linen napkin in his lap.

"Everything looks and smells delicious," he said, smiling and looking at my breasts as I sat down across from him.

"If you think the aroma is wonderful, wait until you taste it."

"You're absolutely right," he said, taking the first bite of his omelet. He closed his eyes and deeply moaned with each and every mouthful. I became intensely aroused as I watched him lick the maple syrup from his thick, juicy lips. I desperately wanted to fuck this man.

"You know what, Jada? I have to come clean," he began.

"Please do," I encouraged as I took a sip of my mimosa.

"Since that day at the dealership, I haven't been able to stop thinking about you."

I know that.

"Do tell."

"Well, I must admit that I was a little thrown off by your aggressiveness in the beginning. I'm not used to that. But the more I thought about the tremendous amount of confidence you obviously have, the more turned on I became. And the panties..."

"What about my panties?"

"Let's just say that I used them for inspiration when I was alone."

"Oh, I see." I giggled.

"Do you need me to help with that," he asked, as I rinsed the dishes after we were done with our meal.

"No. I've got it."

"Are you sure," he softly whispered in my ear as he wrapped his strong arms around my waist, pushing my body against the sink. The hardness of his dick on my ass brought a smile to my face. I knew that the dishes would have to wait until later when I felt the fierce throbbing and a surge of dampness between my legs from his tender kiss on the nape of my neck. Soon, my robe fell to the tiled floor, and I was left standing naked in my kitchen. My desire for Damon grew out of control as he cupped my large breasts, squeezing my nipples with his fingers.

I turned and ripped open his shirt, sending what seemed like a thousand tiny white buttons flying like rockets across the room. My tongue joyfully followed the trail from the silky hairs of his chest to his unmistakable six pack and down to the waist of his pants. His breathing accelerated as I unfastened his pants, letting them drop around his ankles. I opened a cabinet drawer and pulled out a horse and carefully slid it on his ever-expanding rod.

Thank goodness I keep a stash of condoms strategically scattered throughout the house. I can't always count on making it to the bedroom.

I slowly circled the swollen head of his long, thick dick several times with my tongue before deciding to take it in whole.

"Oh shit," he hissed at the vibration he felt when I began to hum with his dick pressed against the back of my throat.

When I sensed that Damon's bomb was about to detonate within my cheeks, I pushed him down onto the rooster patterned rug on the kitchen floor and mounted him like I was the Lone Ranger and he was Trigger. Damon grabbed my ample caramel ass and pushed himself even deeper into my saturated pussy. He took one look at the new design that was etched on my mound and smiled.

"Is that?"

"Yes it is," I answered proudly.

"How in the hell did you get the Cadillac emblem on there?"

"Among other things, I am one hell of an artist."

Truth was, I almost had to go to the emergency room over this one. I was usually pretty good at different designs. My initials were the first project that I tried but that became boring after a while. During my years as a huge LA Lakers fan, Kobe's name adorned the place of honor, after that, it was the Chanel symbol because I have always absolutely adored all things Chanel. But this one had a higher degree of difficulty than I had anticipated and the four cups of coffee that I foolishly drank before I started this mission didn't help. Thank goodness that all of the scars have healed. My next goal is to try to shave the Baby Phat kitty on my kitty.

"What kind of ride do you like, Damon? Do you like it fast and furious or slow and steady," I asked breathlessly.

"I like them both. I'll take whatever you give me. "

I began my slow grind on Damon's steel rod. The look of sheer bliss on his face was exactly what I wanted to see. My breasts were perfectly positioned over his lips and he took full advantage of that by gently nibbling on my diamonds, first one, then the other.

The slick sopping sounds of sweet soulful sex were almost deafening. This moment was even better than I had imagined. I'd had more than a few lovers in my time and some of them were pretty good. But

Damon...goddamn! For about a half of a minute, Damon made me consider throwing in my sassy and single card.

Work me, Damon.

Damon licked his thumb and began to stroke my inflamed clit, causing a whimper of ecstasy to escape my open lips. My movements increasingly became more urgently defined. I couldn't believe how perfectly Damon filled me. I never wanted him to stop working my pussy into frenzy.

"Damon," I purred.

He didn't answer. He just kept on driving me insane with constant mind-numbing pleasure.

"Damon..."

Still, no answer.

It soon came to a point when my body no longer felt as though it belonged to me but instead was under the spell of a voodoo curse that controlled each and every hysterical gyration. My body temperature went from flaming hot to ice cold as I erupted, spilling my nectar all over his pulsating cock. The spasms of my walls seemed to send Damon over the edge. His thrusts became more intense, more animalistic.

"Don't stop, Jada. Keep riding my dick," he panted. "Please, just keep fucking the shit out of me. Please."

My energy was far spent but I had to give Damon exactly what he wanted. There was nothing I loved more than having a man beg for me to take him into another dimension. I bucked wildly and furiously rotated my full hips on his hardness.

Oh my God! Another one. I can't take another one. Give me strength.

I closed my eyes and braced myself for another orgasmic hurricane that was sure to knock me off of my foundation. Damon was on the brink of getting swept away by his own gale force winds.

I have never had a man share a climax with me. I don't know if I can hold on.

Damon's groans grew louder beneath my uncontrollable grind until we both erupted with euphoric satisfaction.

"Damn girl. You fuck the same way that you write," he said.

"What in the hell does that mean?" I asked breathlessly.

"You are bold, sassy, and uninhibited both on paper and in real life."

"So you like?"

"Definitely"

"Are you sure? I know how you feel about being with a woman who is more demure," I teased.

"Yeah, well, I'm always willing to shift gears and try something different."

"You shouldn't worry about shifting your gear, Damon. You should let someone do that for you."

"Do you have anyone in particular in mind for the job?" he asked, stroking my glistening back.

"You know I do."

Damon and I showered together but could not resist the overwhelming urge to sex each other senseless again beneath the warmth of the running water. It was times like these that made me glad that I had invested a few more dollars in an extra-large shower with a sturdy bench because Damon and I damn sure wouldn't be able to get our doggie groove on like this in some little ass stall.

"You know, Damon, at this rate, I'll never get to take you for a ride in my new SUV," I pointed out, as we lay naked in each other's arms after a long day of eating, fucking, and sleeping. The funny thing was, at one point, it seemed as if we did all three at the same time.

"Riding in a brand new Cadillac is nice but it pales in comparison to the ride you gave me today."

"Is that right?" I said, mounting him again. "If you play your cards right, Mr. Cadillac salesman, Ms. Jada James will give you a ride like that as often as you like. Who knows, I may even engrave your name you know where."

Damon and I were great together. He was a hardworking man who never stopped treating me like a lady. We would have endless conversations about everything from the meaning of life to which is the best way to squeeze a tube of toothpaste—from the bottom up or from the center. Laughter was constant when we were together and nothing felt better than having him wrapped around me like a warm blanket on a cold winter's morning. But soon, the familiar yet unwanted marriage conversation came up and Damon did not like what I had to say.

"Jada, I have fallen so deeply in love with everything about you that I can hardly contain myself. The day you walked into my dealership, I saw the sun in the sky shine brighter than I had in my entire life, and I want to keep that in my world forever. I love you, and I want you to be my wife. Why are you so against that?" Damon said, as we cuddled on my couch after attending my publicist's elaborate wedding.

"Damon, what is wrong with what we have now? Why can't we just continue to see each other exclusively? We don't have to be married."

I had indeed grown weary of having this conversation with Damon. I thought that I had made myself clear on this issue.

"Because that is not enough for me, Jada. I want to be more than just your boyfriend or significant other. What is it? Do you think that I wouldn't be a good husband or that I would hurt you in some way?"

"No. That's not it at all. The fact that I don't want to get married has nothing to do with you. I don't want to marry any man and be tied down. You know how it goes. First we'll get married and then after a year or so, you'll start talking about children."

"You say that like it would be the most horrible thing in the world."

"Maybe not for some women but it is for me. Anyway, what difference does it make whether or not you are my husband or my lover? We will still be together."

"It makes a big damn difference! And if you can't understand where I'm coming from on that tip then maybe I need to face the fact that I'm just beating a dead horse."

"What are you saying?" I asked but I already knew what Damon meant. It was the same song that I'd heard whenever a man wanted more than I was willing to give. Marriage was just not an option for me.

"I'm saying that this isn't working for me anymore, Jada. To save my heart from breaking any more than it already has, I need to move on," Damon explained, his voice cracking.

I walked him to the door for the last time. I truly hated to see Damon go but understood why he had too. His passion for marriage wasn't going to go away and neither was my lack thereof.

"Can I at least get a goodbye hug?" I asked with my arms open wide.

He turned, smiled, and retreated into my arms on last time.

I am so going to miss you. I wish I could give you what you want.

"It's been a wonderful ride, Damon Grant, a wonderful ride."

Also by Hazel Mills

MAHOGANY RED BOOKS PRESENTS

AFTER ALL

It was a perfect love until he crossed a line of no return.

A NOVEL BY

HAZEL MILLS

Follow Mahogany Red Books on social media
Twitter @MahoganyRedPub
Instagram @MahoganyRedPub

CPSIA information can be obtained at www.ICGtesting.com
Printed in the USA
LVOW10s2112080416

482788LV00027B/529/P